Pepper Pace

Cover art created by Kim Chambers
Edited by CeCe Monét

PEPPER PACE PUBLICATIONS

ISBN-13: 978-1492853909

Reviews for The Throwaway Year

"A Unique Perspective on Love"
-Nia Forrester, author of Commitment

"This book was different and quirky just like its author Pepper
Pace, but this book makes you look at your self and question what
are you doing to make things better?"
-Dharp APB Perspective Reviews

Dedication

This book is dedicated to YOU; my amazing reader who supports independent authors like myself by purchasing this work and not downloading it illegally. You are loved and appreciated!

My Beata reader Leslie worked tirelessly on this project, as did my editor CeCe Monét. My sister-friend Sue gets props for inspiring my logo and all of the readers and authors on the 2013 IR Romance Cruise Event get much love for being my experimental Betas. If you keep reading, I promise to keep writing.

The Throwaway Year

Table of Contents

"I am perfectly imperfect. I strive for better while loving all that I am today. In loving myself today, I am better equipped to improve myself tomorrow."
-Hayden's Affirmation

"I am more than my past, my mistakes, my faults, my circumstances, my struggles, or my diseases. I am a magnificent totality of imperfect parts only beautified by my choices, bravery and impact."
-Brian's Affirmation

~PROLOGUE~
APRIL 9, 2011

It was Sunday morning and Hayden had no desire to get up and dressed to start her day. The TV was turned on to The Food Network and Paula Deen was cooking something deep-fried, fattening, and more than likely also deadly. Hayden's stomach grumbled--right now she would eat ten of whatever Paula Deen was cooking!

MyKell was laying quietly, eyes staring at the TV screen. He'd been quiet all weekend. "Hey, you want to go to The Cracker Barrel for lunch?" They had lazed through breakfast and now it was early afternoon. MyKell's eyes seemed to flinch. "I'm paying," she interjected before he could object.

MyKell put the cheap in *cheapskate*. He was 42 and had just gotten his first decent paying job since they'd been together. All of his other jobs had been in sales where he barely raked in enough commission to cover his own personal expenses, let alone enough to help her out financially. They had been together for nearly six years, so Hayden knew the routine. If she wanted to go out to eat then it would be *her* treat.

MyKell turned to her slowly. "Hade, I need to talk to you."

Oh shit. He'd lost another job. The hell with this! He'd only been working at the new place for six weeks-

"I met someone else."

Hayden blinked. "What?" Her heart had momentarily frozen in her chest and was now fluttering rapidly against her ribcage. MyKell pulled himself out of the bed, looking like someone had socked him in his stomach instead of the other way around...

1

"I'm sorry, Hade. But things haven't been right for a while...
I'm moving out." He walked to the closet while she stared after
him with her mouth hanging open. *Things hadn't been right for a
while...*

How could he be saying this when they'd just made love last
night? She had picked him up from work Friday and for once
they'd had a good evening. He had allowed her to ramble on and
on about work and her best friend Dani's problems with her man
of the hour. He had actually listened to her intently without
rolling his eyes and stating that he was tired of hearing about her
whiny-ass friends.

Was that why? Was he only being nice to her because he
knew that he was going to do this? Her breath froze in her throat
as she watched him pull on a jogging suit; a 42 year old man that
dressed like a 22 year old in his Sean Jean urban gear and
Timberland boots.

Then like a boomerang, her mind sprang back. This entire
weekend had been fake, just a bone he'd thrown her to ease her
pain. She watched his back thinking, *he has met someone else. He
has fallen in love with someone else. He is not in love with me
anymore...*

Every new thought brought another crashing pain. She was
35 and had given this man six years of her life and now that he
had finally gotten a decent job, he was leaving her. It was her
house that he had moved into because why should two struggling
people have two households? It was also her paycheck that had
kept them fed when he quit a job because it was yet another low
paying job not worth his time. Hayden felt the tears burn the back
of her eyes, but she thought that she would rather die than to let
him see her cry.

She already felt foolish enough. *Things hadn't been right for a
while...* but she hadn't known that. MyKell placed a suitcase on
the bed and began loading things into it. He was talking about
making arrangements to pick up the rest of his things.

She wanted to get up, but she couldn't. Beneath the bed
covers she was still naked and... well, he already had someone

else. How could she let him see her naked when he had another woman? She quickly averted her eyes. She wouldn't look at him because then she would see that tall caramel colored man that she remembered from six years ago; with his toned body and thick curls due to his mixed Black and Hispanic heritage.

Back then she was pushing thirty and convinced that she would never find a man that would want her for more than just a booty call or a stepping stone to something better. So even though now he was a lot less muscular and a whole lot greyer, she didn't see that because he would always be that fine man that had chosen her. Hayden realized that the real reason she couldn't look him in the eyes was because she was afraid that she would see in them just what she really was to him; a fat, short, yellow skinned, freckled face Black woman with kinked out sandy red hair.

"Hayden?" he was talking to her.

"Just take all your things now." Her voice was a whisper even though she was trying to speak normally. She gripped the bed covers and slid to the end of the bed while he watched her with his dark, hurt eyes.

There was a pile of clothes on the floor; hers, his. She picked up the panties that she'd shed the night before and pulled them over her big thighs, knowing that he could see the crack of her ass when she bent over. She quickly put on yesterdays jeans and a t-shirt, both were dirty, but it at least didn't require her to walk across the room to the dresser for something fresh.

She dressed quickly wondering when he had met her; this other woman. Was it someone he worked with? Someone she knew? She wasn't going to watch him walk out the door because... yes, he was the one leaving her, but she wouldn't watch him do it!

The tears were running down her face suddenly, but she kept her head down so that he wouldn't see. She would die if he saw her crying. He'd used her, faked it with her, but when he left, she would at least still have her dignity.

"I'm going to leave now. When I come back... if you could just not be here..." Then she hurried out of the room and down

3

the hall as the first sob forced its way from her mouth and the hot tears blurred her vision, dripping down her face and from her chin. She grabbed her purse and slipped on flip-flops and then she was hurrying out of the house and to her car. MyKell didn't have a car but... well, he had someone else and *she* probably had one. Yeah, chances are, she would have one.

Hayden started her car and pulled out of her driveway without looking. Thank God she lived on a residential street that saw very little traffic, or she might have been hit. She gripped the steering wheel as the tears and sobs wracked her body. Her chest ached when she thought about the six years and how easily he'd been able to say that he'd found someone else. Even after all that she had done for him...

Knowing that it wasn't safe for her to continue driving, Hayden pulled into the nearest place where she could safely lose it. It was the parking lot of a Kroger's grocery store. After she was safely stopped, she stared at herself in the mirror, not recognizing the ugly woman that looked back at her. Hatred bubbled up inside of her, but it was all directed at herself.

She hated her too light skin with its freckles scattered across her nose. Red bone. High yella – but not pretty, she didn't have the long flowing hair or the limber body that most people associated with light skinned females. When she looked at herself she simply saw an out of shape woman with a Don King mess of hair covering her head. When she reached up to wipe her blotchy face of its tears and snot she smelled her unwashed body. She averted her eyes in disgust.

~Chapter 1~
GETTING RIGHT WITH SELF

Hayden was staring at the phone number that MyKell had left on a slip of paper. When she'd returned *that* day, MyKell had been gone but there had been a brief note telling her that if she needed to contact him for her to call him on his cell phone. Then she'd seen a new number there, one that probably belonged to his new cell phone that was probably provided by his new girlfriend.

Hayden felt herself frowning. She could stand here, staring at this phone number for hours speculating about what the two of them were doing together right now, or how many times had they made love since he'd left, how many times he had called her baby... She felt another spike of hurt before it dwindled down into a dull ache. The phone rang and she hurried to it, almost picking it up before the first ring had ended. She stilled her hand and let it ring twice more before she slowly answered.

"Hello?" she tried not to sound hopeful.

"Hayden? You okay girl? You haven't been to work in two days and I was getting worried." It was her best friend Danyelle; Dani. She didn't answer. The disappointment that it wasn't *him* was just too strong. "Do you want me to come over? Hade?"

"I'm okay." She mumbled. "I just, need some time alone." Dani sighed, but after a moment gave a reluctant goodbye. Staring at the phone receiver, Hayden wondered just how long she was going to do this. How long was she going to rehash this betrayal, this hurt? Why couldn't this part be over already? If she could just go to sleep and wake up and it could be a year later — because then, in a year she could be skinny *and* over *him*. If there was only some way to throw this year away...

5

Hayden hung up the phone when it began to beep loudly and then walked into her kitchen. Her feet carried her automatically to the refrigerator before she brought herself to a stumbling halt. She blinked in disbelief at how automatic it was to open the refrigerator and to place food into her mouth without even realizing it. She had sworn to herself that she was going to go on a diet and straighten herself up — but she couldn't stay disciplined for even one day!

She looked around almost amazed at how she was living. There were unwashed dishes in the sink from the week before! Her floors needed sweeping, her laundry needed doing, her bathroom needed cleaning... but more importantly she was a hot mess; and not just physically. Her credit was a mess from indulging in her and MyKell's every whim. She needed to get right with herself; outside and in.

Hayden gritted her teeth and stormed to the sink where she filled it with hot soapy water. Almost frantically, she began to clean. Sweat ran down her body in rivulets as she moved through her house like a cleaning tornado.

Hayden did not stop moving until after 2:00 A.M. and by that time her floors were mopped and waxed, her furniture glowed with orange oil, her bathroom was scrubbed and sparkling, and her laundry was washed, folded and put away. She stripped out of her clothes, averting her eyes as she passed the mirror and stepped into her shower. She scrubbed her body and her hair but when she stepped from the bath wrinkled like a prune she felt just as dirty as she had when she had entered it.

Exhausted, Hayden slipped into her crisp clean sheets, falling asleep almost as quickly as her head touched her pillow. When she woke up the next morning, the idea that had taken root in her head wouldn't leave. She stared at the ceiling feeling the empty gnawing in her stomach — what others called hunger, but what she knew was really just an excuse to bury her pain in food.

She climbed out of bed slowly, her body sore and stiff from the impromptu workout. She picked up her telephone to call in sick yet another day, and not because she wanted to sit around and mope, but because she had a plan. Hayden walked over to the calendar that hung behind the door. April 12, 2011.

Why shouldn't she throw away the next year of her life, especially if it was to get right with herself? She had given six years to a man with no ambition, no drive and obviously no loyalty. So why shouldn't she just devote one year of her life to better herself; regardless of how much discomfort it gave her or how unpleasant it was? One year to become a new person...otherwise she would always be this woman that she had grown to hate.

Hayden returned to her bed and made it up neatly. No more messes. She had to get her house in order, her finances straight and of course she had to get right with herself.

After getting dressed she went to the supermarket and loaded the cart with healthy and nutritious food. She had always hated the taste of low fat anything and she would choose tepid water over an iced cold drink sweetened with fake sugar. Diets worked for a while, until she ended all of her hard work with a slice of cake and buffalo chicken wings. Or her daily cup of coffee loaded with whipped cream and caramel.

Hayden knew the foods that would help her to lose weight— and she knew the diets that were the most successful because she had tried them all. She just couldn't stick with anything unpleasant; including exercise, tasteless food, and denying herself some small pleasure. Hayden stared sadly at a display of Krispy Kreme doughnuts.

Heated for a few seconds in the microwave, and then dunked into a steaming cup of coffee, that was one of her favorite treats... Wait, she couldn't tolerate unpleasant things? She had tolerated her own gluttony and lack of drive. *What do you want more Hade; doughnuts or to be someone that you can be proud of?*

With a decisive nod, Hayden walked past the doughnuts. As she was loading her groceries into her car, she spotted a Quick Cuts in the strip mall across the street. She touched her ponytail, which didn't even capture all of her split ends. Then she hurried across the street and stepped into the small shop. All eyes were on her until a stylish white woman whisked her away to a chair, a look of horror on her face as she studied Hayden's head. Hayden just shrugged inwardly.

"Cut it off."

"All of it?"

"Leave me an inch." That was about the amount of her new growth. The hairdresser nodded in relief that she wasn't going to be given the task of flat ironing, curling, or otherwise trying to make her sandy kinks halfway acceptable. Hayden wouldn't miss it. The hair was over processed, dry, and pretty much beyond repair anyway.

After the cut, what was left curled softly with the help of proper moisturizers. The woman commented that it looked good, and it was the truth. Yet, Hayden just nodded. It didn't matter if it looked good. The point was to get rid of the bad so that there would be room for the good.

After leaving the strip mall and taking her groceries home, Hayden headed to a local gym. It was less than five miles from her house, which meant that she should be able to go to the gym even on a whim. In the past, she had always put off joining this gym because it was too hot to be working out, or it was too cold to be driving to a gym. However, the truth was that she just didn't want to look like a fat ass. Ignoring the sight of the toned bodies as well as the not so toned ones, Hayden walked up to the receptionist desk.

"I want a one-year membership, and I need a personal trainer, please. How much will that cost?" The receptionist gave the woman a surprised look as if thinking that fish didn't generally jump onto the hook.

"Let me get a member's representative." Hayden nodded. This was going to be one easy sale...

A buff Black man approached her with a folder in his hand. After introducing himself, he had her sit at a table where he proceeded to try to talk her into buying a membership. Hayden interrupted him.

"Sold. Explain what's in the fine print and then tell me where to sign." The man stuttered and then smiled broadly. Moments later they were shaking hands.

The price of the membership was on promotion and very fair, but it would still stretch her finances and didn't even include a personal trainer, since the facility only had employees who showed the members how to work the machinery. Then the sales rep explained that many personal trainers were members who brought their clients here to workout. The man looked around while Hayden watched him discreetly, wishing that he was a personal trainer. Not that she was the least bit interested in him, but his body appeared to be as close to perfect as humanly possible.

He waved his hand to a group of body builders lifting weights in front of a huge mirror. "Todd!"

The person that turned was far from the hulking figure of the other men. Todd jogged over to them. He was a White man of average height and build. Hayden couldn't see much of his physique as he wore workout pants and a loose fitting shirt.

"Todd, this is Hayden Michaels. She's looking for a personal trainer."

He shook her hand. "Hi, I'm Todd Crandle."

"*You're* a personal trainer?"

He just chuckled, not appearing offended by her apparent lack of confidence.

"Not just a personal trainer; I'm NCSF certified. I also have a Bachelor's of Science degree in Physical Fitness. But best of all, I'm not just some muscle head that wants to turn you into a female version of himself."

Hayden's head tilted as she digested his words, deciding that she liked what he had to say. Then the sales rep excused himself when he saw that Hayden had warmed to the idea of Todd.

"I have to warn you though," Todd continued. "I'm also a fulltime Firefighter and I just recently got married, so my schedule is pretty hectic. So if you're willing to work around my craziness, then I'll give you a break on my usual fee."

She perked up even more at that and discovered that Todd worked a 24-hour shift at the firehouse, and then had the next 48 hours off. She was far from rich, so it helped that he would cut her a break. So Hayden agreed to his terms.

Then they decided to meet at the end of the week at the butt crack of dawn. Todd insisted that she get a physical first and though it had been years since she had seen a doctor, it was just another thing that she needed to do in order to get right with herself. After leaving the gym, Hayden checked off a mental list in her head.

She picked up a newspaper and then headed for a small café. When the waitress asked her what she wanted to order, she indicated a cup of hot tea with lemon and a grilled chicken Cesar salad. Then she searched the want ads, circling several perspective part time jobs. She needed to get her finances together, and to do that she needed another job.

~Chapter 2~
GETTING TO THE MONEY

I value my health, as I can't truly love myself without loving and inner-adorning the shine that encapsulates the magic of my soul.

Hayden stared at the words that she had written across her calendar. Did she believe the words? No... and that was pretty pathetic.

Her doctor's visit had not gone well — not well at all.

"Aren't you feeling... sick?" he had asked her with squinted eyes as he scrutinized her. She just shrugged and shook her head.

"Well Miss Michaels once you begin taking this medication you will realize that you were indeed sick..." he smiled, "because you will begin to feel tons better."

Hayden took her morning dose of diabetes, high blood pressure and high cholesterol medicine. Well... at least she now had a doctor's note for why she had taken damn near a week off from work. *See Boss Lady, I'm not just mooning away because some man dumped me. I'm really sick! Check out my A1C level. I should be freaking dead...*

Hayden pulled on sweat pants. They were MyKell's... well, they had been until he snagged them on a nail and wouldn't wear them once they were damaged goods. She found scissors and shortened the legs so that she wouldn't trip on them and then pulled on one of MyKell's undershirts. It was like a dress on her. With a frown, she shook her head and then prepared her breakfast; oatmeal, sugar substitute with soymilk. It nearly turned her stomach, but apparently, it was a healthy diabetic breakfast; one that she would have to tolerate for the next year at least... *360 more days and counting.*

When Hayden pulled into the gym parking lot and it was 5:29 A.M. She dashed through the doors expecting it to be completely empty except for Todd, but there were a few die-hard workout enthusiasts apparently doing what she had in mind; a workout before heading to the job.

"Good morning," Todd greeted her sounding chipper. He was holding a cup of coffee, which she eyed wantonly, but no coffee for her. Her caffeine addiction would take at least a full week to kick.

Todd had her get on the treadmill first.

"Aren't I supposed to stretch first, or something-?" She looked warily at the machine, images of fat women falling off them and being posted to YouTube instantly started swirling around her mind...

"Only if you want a muscle or ligament tear. Always warm up before stretching."

Okay, that made sense. So she stepped on the treadmill and he started it at a moderate walk. She started to sweat five minutes into the walk. Ten minutes into it, her heart began thumping and she wondered what she was going to do when he made her run? He was quiet as he studied her file and then took her pulse while she struggled to maintain her balance and speed.

"Good. What did you eat this morning?"

Did he really expect her to talk when she could barely breathe? "Oatmeal," she managed.

"Good."

After fifteen minutes, he allowed her to stop. She wanted to drop to the floor, but waited patiently for his next instructions instead. They did some stretching which felt really good and then Todd took her through an upper body circuit. The weights were very small, not very heavy at all, and she felt that she could go much heavier. Until he took her through several repetitions and then she wanted to beg him to stop.

She didn't stop and she didn't complain. Todd explained each step of the way until she understood how to work through each exercise slowly so that her muscles would feel the burn. To think she had always tried to avoid the burn not realizing that muscles had to break down so that they could rebuild themselves stronger too. Maybe that was just a universal truth... The hour finally came to an end and Hayden wanted nothing more than to go home and climb into bed; but she couldn't. She had to finally return to work.

"I want you to do this exact same thing every other day until I start you on lower body. You need to walk more to improve your cardio so take stairs when possible, okay?"

"Yes," she nodded.

He smiled at her. "Good job. I'll see you Sunday afternoon."

Hayden's plan had been to do an hour workout each morning before heading to her job in hopes that she would feel invigorated throughout the day. However, the reality is that she was far from invigorated. Her body began to ache in places where she didn't even know she had muscles.

She entered her office building and bypassed the elevator and headed for the stairs which would take her to the fourth floor. Todd told her to do it and she said she would. Period. It took her three times as long to get to her office and she was sweating and out of breath but in some ways each aching step felt like... rebirth.

She grudgingly admitted that the pain and the ache felt kind of good; not physically but mentally. It was pain that was killing away the bad and creating something new and not pain based on what someone else had done to her. It was the pain of success...

"Oh my God, Hayden!" Dani exclaimed when Hayden came panting and limping over to her cubicle. She fell into her office chair, which squeaked loudly and she hoped it wouldn't break on her, because if she hit the floor she wasn't sure she would be able to get back up.

"Girl... what in the world...? Wow your hair looks good."

Hayden blinked at her in surprise. She patted her TWA – teeny weeny afro, and then shrugged. She dug in her purse for her doctor's note. "Dani, be a friend and give this to Boss Lady."

"Of course."

She signed onto her computer. 7:59 A.M. She had made it to work on time. So this was doable. *Ugh…*

"Are you… okay? I've been worried about you. You just disappeared." Dani spoke while they sat in the break room at lunch.

Hayden felt bad that she hadn't done anything to alleviate Dani's concerns. Yet, she didn't know how to explain what she was going through either. How did she tell someone that she wasn't completely detaching herself from anything that might cause her to feel or to want? That it was not a bad thing because if she examined her wants it would only lead to a cup of coffee with whipped cream and — *stop*!

She decided to keep it simple. "I wasn't feeling so hot. So I visited my doctor and guess what? I have diabetes, high blood pressure *and* high cholesterol."

"Damn, Hade…"

"I know. But I decided to get healthy. I joined a gym and I even got a personal trainer."

"*You* joined a gym?" Dani's face was full of surprise. Both women were overweight, but on Dani they called it voluptuous. Her friend was gorgeous with her thick hourglass figure, smooth mocha skin and long extensions.

Dani had actually done a lot to help Hayden realize that being overweight didn't make you unattractive. Dani easily had fifty extra pounds on her tall frame but she also had hips that men couldn't stop looking at and curves that looked good in her clothes. She regularly scheduled trips to the salon to keep her nails and hair perfectly done. Her makeup was always flawless and she had confidence that came with accepting all of herself. Confidence equaled beauty...

Hayden gazed at her confident, beautiful friend. She knew that she couldn't expect a woman like Dani to understand what it was like to have so much self-loathing that making sure she didn't fail was more important than any discomfort she was sure to experience in the course of her self-improvement during this next year. So Hayden plastered on a false smile instead. "I just need to take better care of myself," and then Dani nodded in acceptance.

Hayden speared a lettuce leaf not minding that there was barely enough of the fat free dressing to taste. If she tasted it she might spew anyway...

"Have you heard from *that* man?"

Hayden shook her head slowly. "He's coming this weekend to pick up the last of his things."

"You should put his shit out on the curb-"

"Dani-"

"You were too nice to that loser!"

"Lets not talk about him." She met her friend's eyes. "That part of my life is over. It's all about me now."

"True. Well then let's go out this weekend. I'll take you out to dinner so you won't have to be there when *he's* there."

"No, I have no intentions of being there, but I do have plenty of other things that I need to take care of. Thanks though."

Dani looked a little disappointed but she patted her friend on the shoulder. "You know I'm here if you need me, right?"

"I know. Thanks, but I'm good."

After work Hayden headed to a job interview where she hoped to get a job cleaning a small office complex. It would work well with her schedule in that she would be able to make her own hours. The cleaning just needed to be completed by the following morning.

She was immediately hired after the manager gave a cursory look at the area of her job application that indicated she did not have a criminal history. She was to start Monday evening, five days a week. It would give her an extra grand a month. Not much, but it would pay down her maxed out credit cards and leave her the weekend to devote to herself.

When Hayden finally stumbled into the house later that evening, she grabbed the calendar from the bedroom and placed it on the refrigerator using a magnetic clip. She read the self-affirmation again. *I value my health, as I can't truly love myself without loving and inner-adorning the shine that encapsulates the magic of my soul…*

If Hayden experienced even one moment of happiness in the following week, she could not recollect it. To anyone other than to her personal trainer or Dani, she barely spoke a word. Todd increased her treadmill time to twenty minutes, which she maintained each morning even when he wasn't there. She then went to work nearly bent in pain and at lunch ate a salad or sandwich.

After working her first job, she then drove to the office complex where she had three offices to clean. It took every bit of four hours so if she wanted to get to bed at a decent hour she had to hustle. She particularly disliked cleaning the large office on the first floor with its big plate glass window overlooking the parking lot. The people who occupied that office worked late and so it was always her last stop. On top of that, they were foul people who left a horrible mess.

Her routine included wiping out the water fountain where there was always grit in it like someone had dumped coffee grounds down the drain. She dumped the trashcans of each cubicle and filled them with new plastic liners. She dusted, vacuumed and then mopped and cleaned both sets of bathrooms.

Yet what was even worse than even cleaning two filthy bathrooms was cleaning the little canteen.

Each day she would see the tables littered with used food wrappers and overflowing ashtrays. She knew why no one threw away their trash—because the cans were just small ones that were used in the cubicles and they just overflowed. Still there was no excuse for why they left the microwave in the condition that she found it in each night. It would take forever for her to scrub the burnt crud or sticky goo from the tray and walls.

The first night that she had cleaned away a month's worth of old food; she had stepped back and looked at the sparkling clean microwave with pride. Now that she had taken the first step they would surely cover their food, wipe up their spills, and keep it clean. However, when she returned the next day, there was macaroni and cheese stuck in it and someone had microwaved something red that had splattered and dried all over the interior. Hayden closed her eyes and counted to ten.

I train myself to focus on positive thoughts so the fruits produced by my subconscious are ripe and rich instead of weeds that devour and swallow... She had to repeat that affirmation three times before she was calm enough to re-clean all that she had meticulously cleaned the night before. At first when she had scanned her computer for self-affirmations, which could be repeated during moments of weakness or self-doubt, she thought they would just be frivolous words that she wouldn't be able to relate to. Although in truth, she really couldn't totally relate to them, she said them anyway because she hoped that one day she would believe them.

By the time she finally dragged herself back to her home, she seldom did anything but bathe and fall into bed. It was a good trade off. Though she was tired and sore each night, she was also too busy to think about MyKell.

He had come by to pick up his things the weekend before, just as his phone message had indicated. Only she wasn't there to witness it—when she returned home, there was simply an absence of his remaining remnants. His key lay on the dining room table and she tossed it into the garbage.

She would call a locksmith the next day and get all of the locks changed. Then Hayden had walked through her clean home taking stock and if she found something that reminded her of MyKell, she threw it in the garbage, including the workout pants and t-shirt that had once belonged to him. Instead of feeling sad or hurt, now she just felt closure.

By the end of week two, Hayden had returned to the doctor and found that she had lost nine pounds. Todd was happy about it, but she felt that it should have been more. She had worked hard and though her pants were a bit baggier, she still thought she looked like the same unkempt fat woman. She barely even looked in the mirror; she had trained herself to see only the things that she needed to in order to not walk around with lettuce stuck in her teeth or toilet paper hanging from the back of her pants.

Todd's way of celebrating her accomplishments was to allow her to leave the treadmill but she now had to use the recumbent bike for half an hour. Somehow she thought that by sitting it would be easier, but that was not true. The weekend was the only time that Hayden had for herself. After she gave Todd his pound of flesh on Saturday or Sunday, she took care of cleaning her home, paying bills, or visiting with Dani. Then it was time to prepare for the upcoming week; preparing her meals, getting her clothes together so that she wouldn't have to dash around wondering what to wear when she had not a minute to spare in the morning, and not an ounce of energy left in the evening.

She had her life regulated down to the minute. It allowed her sweet emptiness, mindless activity where she had no time to think about anything beyond the task at hand. It was hard, but it was also slowly healing her.

Time might heal old wounds—but so did focusing on something more unpleasant like knotted muscles, a grumbling belly and total exhaustion. The only thing she couldn't quite regulate was the last office that she had to clean each night. At times they worked until 10:00 P.M. and she had to sit in her car silently stewing that she wouldn't be in bed until midnight.

It wouldn't do her any good to clean while they were still present if they were going to refill the ashtrays that she'd just cleaned, or piss on the floor of the restroom that she'd just mopped! To say that she was annoyed by it all would be an understatement. A few times, she had even fallen asleep behind her steering wheel, which was bad. Yet worse was when her mind would begin to wander back to MyKell.

~Chapter 3~
THE BOILER ROOM

Hayden watched the lady with the 1950s' bouffant hairstyle leave the office, using her key to lock up. Stifling a yawn, Hayden brushed past the older woman who gave her a suspicious look. Hayden used her own janitorial service issued key to unlock the just locked door, ignoring the woman who had stopped to watch her as she entered the large office.

Hayden moved quickly, dumping the trash and huffing under her breath. When these people left their cubicles for the night, they also left half eaten food and drinks on their desks and they left their chairs almost halfway out into the aisle. Well she wasn't supposed to touch anything on anyone's desk—even if it was a bunch of sticky napkins from where someone had made a half-hearted attempt to clean up a spill.

It gave her a new appreciation for her own workstation at her fulltime job. Now she made double sure to keep the liner in place and to push her chair up to her desk at the end of the day. There were 26 cubicles in this office and it took a chunk of the night to get all of the chairs pushed up to their desks so that she could get to her vacuuming. Of the 26 cubicles, there were three that remained neat and she was grateful that some people had apparent home training.

She hadn't been the least bit curious about what they did here. She knew a boiler room when she saw one. They were a bunch of telemarketers. How many similar places had she dropped off or picked up MyKell from? Jobs like this had a high turn around so who cared if the carpet under your feet was stained, especially when the guy sitting next to you was probably

20

living out of his car and hadn't bathed in days? Telemarketing was a job of fast money and lots of... *sitting*.

Contemplating her sore hamstrings, Hayden suddenly thought of a solution. She returned to the manager's office that she had just cleaned. She tried reading the faded stenciling on the outside of the door but FOX, VINYL, and A S was all that she could make out. So she snooped around the messy desk only long enough to write down the phone number and name of the company.

Cleaning this pigsty wasn't worth the small amount of pay that she was getting. Maybe she would fare better working sales. MyKell had done it for years and she knew the ends and outs of it, though she'd never sold anything in her life. Yet if MyKell could do it, then she sure as hell could too. So the next day, Hayden called the owner of the company, Robert Fox. He gave her an impromptu interview over the phone.

"You have a very pleasant phone voice Miss Michaels. I understand that you've never done sales before, but we have a script and I think you will do fine. If you like, you can begin tomorrow, and I see no reason why you wouldn't be able to work later in the evening. After all, we have customers on the West coast. Miss Michaels, welcome aboard."

"Mr. Fox I have to give two weeks notice. Would it be a problem if I started after that?" She had considered just quitting her cleaning job with no notice but this place was just way too nasty not to make sure that the cleaning company found someone to replace her.

There was a brief hesitation. "I think we can work with you on that."

"Thank you Mr. Fox." Hayden hung up pleased as she did a mental calculation of how much she was sure to make at the higher paying position.

Two weeks later, she was walking through the door of the same office complex that she had been cleaning for the last month and a half. However, this time, the office was a bustle with activity. She paused inside of the door as 19 sets of eyes met hers. 18 sets of eyes turned away, quickly dismissing her. She looked at the one person that hadn't looked away. It was someone sitting at one of the tidy desks; one of the few people here with home training.

Or... maybe not. He stared at her with dispassionate grey eyes as he talked on the phone, and the polite head nod that she was about to give him was quickly abandoned at his rude stare. Hayden headed to the back of the room where Mr. Fox's office was located. She knocked on the door now understanding that the faded stenciling read: "FOX VINYL AND MAP ADS."

"Come," said a gruff voice from inside, which sounded nothing like the polished man that she had spoken to over the phone two weeks before. Mr. Fox was holding an ink pen, which was poised over a document. His eyes swept over her body before settling on her face.

"Hayden Michaels?" he asked. He was sixtyish, fit and not totally unpleasant to look at.

She moved forward and offered her hand. "Yes. I'm Hayden Michaels." He stood and accepted her hand. After a polite exchange of greetings he had her sit in a plastic chair before his desk. He spent the next half hour "training" her and then showed her to an empty desk out in the main room.

Ah. It was the second neat desk in the room. No wonder... it was empty. She glanced over at the third neat desk and noted that it too was empty. Her faith in mankind once again diminished.

"Pam will be your on-the-job coach. If you have any questions, just ask her, though it is very simple and I don't think you will have any problems."

Hayden hid her doubts. That half hour discussion in his office wasn't very much in the way of training. When she looked over at her OJ coach, whose workstation was right next to hers, she saw the little old bouffant lady from the other week. The

22

woman appeared to be in her late fifties with painted on eyebrows and crimson lipstick. Yikes. Pam gave her the once over before plastering a fake smile on her thin wrinkled lips.

She walked over to Hayden and offered her hand. Hayden accepted it, shaking it carefully as she was so thin that it felt like she had the bones of a little bird.

"Aren't you our cleaning lady?" Pam asked loudly. Mr. Fox raised his brow in surprise.

Hayden found herself already disliking Pam. "Not anymore," she responded.

"Oh, I didn't realize that you... um worked here before." Mr. Fox interjected and Hayden wanted to say that it would have been on her application if he had asked her for one.

"So you didn't like it, huh?" Pam asked with a smirk. Hayden suddenly wished that she could skip this part too; where she was expected to be nice to people simply because they were her co-workers. Where she also had to politely listen to them share stories about their tedious lives.

Hayden could feel her build up of tension suddenly disperse as she decided that there was absolutely no reason why she had to be that person. This was about getting to the money, and there was no time to expend on friendship, foolishness, or frivolity. So she gave Pam a neutral look.

"I'm Hayden Michaels and I understand that you will be my... OJ coach? Mr. Fox gave me some information but I have some questions if you don't mind?"

Pam sniffed when it appeared that she couldn't needle the new girl. "Oh... sure." Mr. Fox left them to it, retreating back to his office. As soon as he was gone, Pam's pleasant smile disappeared.

"You can double jack with me and listen to how I do things. Just watch what I do. You and I will be working the back half of the Detroit phonebook. There's a copy of last year's on the floor over there."

Pam returned to her desk and pretty much disregarded Hayden as she went about making her next call. Hayden retrieved the phonebook from a messy pile on the floor. The pile contained phonebooks from different cities; Norfolk, Columbus and then she saw Detroit. She grabbed it, finally seeing the vinyl cover where she would sale ad space.

It was covered front and back with ads for businesses, restaurants, hotels, etc. She noted that there was a clipboard hanging on the wall near Pam's desk with a mock up of a phonebook cover. Looking around the room, she spotted other clipboards with their own mock-up phonebook covers for the cities that were being called by the other telemarketers. It clicked into place when she saw people periodically jump up to jot initials or check marks on them indicating which ad space had been sold on the covers for the cities that they were calling.

Hayden opened the box that Mr. Fox had given her containing a new headset which she put together quickly before wheeling her chair to Pam's workstation. Pam pointed to a place on her phone where Hayden could plug in to listen to the conversation; double jack. The older women didn't offer her any explanation of what she was doing as she rapidly flitted around the script and fired amounts to her customers—amounts that were different than the ones listed in the script given to Hayden.

When that call ended, Pam picked up her copy of the yellow pages that lay sprawled on her desk and scanned it without bothering to tell Hayden what she was looking for. Hayden knew from MyKell that this was called cold calling. When telemarketers don't have a lead, they have to cold call.

Pam began the process over, asking if the caller wanted to advertise on the vinyl phonebook cover and then discussing how much the ads would cost. If the customer seemed uninterested, she then chopped the price down, and if there still was no interest, Pam grumbled a half hearted goodbye and hung up. After about half an hour of this, she stood up and announced that she needed a cigarette.

Pam didn't invite Hayden to join her and just walked away to go to the canteen. Hayden was too busy jotting down notes to care. Once Pam was gone, it gave Hayden the freedom to pick up the woman's order forms that were to go to the printers.

It was just a mess of crossed out amounts and circled names and she could not make hide nor hair of it, so she disregarded it wondering if she might have actually been better off staying the cleaning woman. Then Hayden scanned through the training material that Mr. Fox had given her and found a list of ad sizes with price amounts. Based on what the board indicated, more than half of their cover had already been sold. She tuned to the other people in the room, listening to what they were doing, and in that way, Hayden began to teach herself how to sell advertisement space on a phonebook cover.

~Chapter 4~
PRETTY GIRLS

Todd was on the treadmill right next to her bike and he was pounding away at a full out run. Hayden had been pedaling for 30 minutes and he had not slowed his pace once. She had long since stopped equating Todd's fitness with his muscle size. The man was a freaking rock!

Wiry muscles lined his arms and he often times wore loose fitting shorts that did little to conceal thundering legs and a boulder butt. Long ago she had considered him to be an Average Joe that looked a little like that actor Adrien Brody — well Adrien Brody with a hyped up body. Not a bad combination in her opinion, but she now gave him much more credit in the looks department.

However, Hayden's appreciation of Todd's looks was no indication of any type of romantic notion. Her trainer was quite obviously in love with his wife and her two sons from a previous relationship. Besides, the idea of love just made Hayden feel cold.

After another five minutes of rapid pedaling, Hayden managed to throw him a scowl. "What are you doing, trying to show me up?"

Todd gave her a sheepish look and slowed his run to a fast walk. "Sorry. I decided to do the Zombie Run this year. I haven't jogged in a while and I need to get back into condition."

She snorted. "*Back* in condition?"

"Well, runner's condition." He pressed stop on the treadmill and hopped off.

"I was just kidding Todd. Don't stop running," she huffed breathlessly as she continued pedaling. "You're giving me motivation to keep pushing it. Notice that I passed the thirty minute point?"

He looked at the time on her bike and smiled. "Damn girl – you go!"

She smiled proudly.

"Ten more minutes and then you can stop."

"Wha-?"

"You can do it, Hayden. That will put you at forty-five minutes."

She would throw up before she got to 45 minutes... but she didn't. With pride, she climbed off the bike ten minutes later while Todd gave her a loud applause.

"Hayden, do you realize that you can now ride a bike non-stop for twelve full miles?"

Her hands were resting on her bent knees as she tried to find her breath. She watched fat drops of sweat hit the floor with a soft yet repetitive *ping*. She lifted her head to look at him, causing the rivulets of sweat to run down her neck. "What's a Zombie Run?"

"Come on; let's walk before you tighten up." As they made a circuit around the gym, Todd explained that each fall his fire department hosted a 50K marathon where the participants dressed as zombies.

"Fifty K?"

"That's just over thirty-one miles." His head snapped back around to her. "You know what Hayden, you should join it."

She made a rude noise with her mouth.

"No, seriously. You just did twelve miles without stopping."

"But I was riding a bike-"

"It doesn't matter. It's still cardio."

She gave him a doubtful look. "I don't think I can run for thirty-one miles."

"Not even if zombies were chasing you?"

She smiled.

Todd stopped walking and gave her a serious look. "Hayden... I don't mean to pry but... well; you don't seem to take much pride in your accomplishments." Hayden's mouth opened to protest, but Todd stopped her. "I know you're working hard and really pushing yourself, but do you realize the great strides that you've made in the last two months?"

She looked at him with confusion. "I'm still shaped exactly the same, even if I have lost a couple of pounds."

He shook his head. "You're a work in progress, but you're not the same. You can do forty-five minutes of cardio, and that's nothing to sneeze at. Look, I would never suggest you do something that I knew you couldn't. I believe that I can get you in condition to run a fifty K."

She considered his words and thought about how she could now walk up the four flights of stairs to her job each morning without breathing hard. Also, how she had tightened the drawstring on her workout pants to keep them from dropping down her smaller hips.

"Okay," she said slowly. The idea of running a marathon— hell just running in general, scared her, but... "Yeah, I'll try it."

He smiled and clapped her on her shoulder. "Awesome. We'll start training at our next session."

Hayden dragged ass into her second job later that evening, grateful that she would be sitting for the next four hours. This was her third day as a Telemarketer and she had yet to sell one ad. Yet at least she now understood some things better. The entire room was split into sales teams; hers seeming to be a band of misfits that all of the other teams had probably rejected like the kids in school that no one picked to be on their dodge ball team.

They consisted of Pam, who hadn't said more then ten words to her all week. She smoked in excess and Hayden was happy that there was a policy that all smoking had to be done in the canteen, which meant that Pam had to leave the area every half an hour to feed her nicotine addiction. Next on her team was the rude guy with the neat desk.

From what Hayden could make out, his name was Brian, although Pam was the only one who had called him by his name. Pam had actually said "Brine" like he was something she soaked a turkey in. This was Covington, Kentucky though, so the room was filled with varying forms of countrified and Mid-Western dialects.

Then there was Marcus, an older Black man that smoked weed in his car during his breaks and lunch. He would always give himself away by returning with red eyes and singing doo-wop songs, or blasting jokes that made no sense. Last was Abdullah, who was of some unidentifiable race and who had an unidentifiable accent. He complained all the time and smelled funny.

Well, she was sure that they had some equally unappealing thoughts about her; *the new hire... you know the pig-faced Black lady with freckles.* Or maybe they laughed at her fruitless attempts to make a sale, stumbling over her words and getting hung up on while she was in the middle of a sentence. It didn't matter what anyone else thought though. She had decided that she would keep to herself during her four-hour shift and had made no attempts to be friendly with anyone here. This was a throwaway year and nothing that happened during it would mean anything except getting right with herself.

She placed her purse into her desk drawer before noticing that all of the sales had been removed from the mock up cover on her team's clipboard. She glanced at the open phonebook on Pam's desk. As usual Pam was off in the canteen smoking and drinking coffee. They had apparently finished Detroit and were now working Kansas City. Someone had placed a new phonebook on her uncluttered desk and she smiled. Yes, a fresh start with a new book!

Hayden stiffened her resolve as she sat down and studied her copy of the yellow pages sheathed in the previous years vinyl cover. She was going to make a sale if it killed her because there was no way that she would allow Pam to out sale her with her hacker's cough that marked the end of nearly every one of her sentences. Besides, no one was following the stupid script that she had been given, so why should she?

Hayden looked at the ads that had previously sold coming up with a great idea. She would start calling them. They had already purchased, right? Chances were they would be interested again, and at the very least they would be an easy sale.

There was a 5x9 ad that took up a huge amount of space on the back cover. She would get 30% commission from each sale... that would net her $156 for selling just that one ad. Hayden picked up her telephone, checking the time difference and decided that it wasn't too late to call these businesses.

"Hello, this is Hayden Michaels of Fox Vinyl and Map Ads. May I speak to the person in charge of your advertisements?"

The man who answered indicated he was in charge of marketing and advertisement. Hayden explained that his automotive company had advertised on the city's vinyl phonebook cover the year before and she was interested in whether he would like to advertise again.

"Is this with the Chamber of Commerce?"

"Uh... no," she responded.

"Well, we're working with the Chamber this year-"

"Oh well you know Fox Vinyl has exclusive access to vinyl covers in your area. Anyone who scans the phonebook looking for automotive repairs will see your glossy ad right there before they even open the book."

"Well..."

"Also, you have one of the better spots on the cover which we did save for your company. We just began our new campaign and I would hate to see it go to one of your competitors." Hayden held her breath and crossed her fingers... *and* toes. *Please, please, please...*

"Hmmm... Well, how much is it?"

"It's five-hundred and twenty dollars, which will get you a full year of advertisement, your name and logo in color with space for your phone and fax numbers, as well as your hours of operation and a line or two that you can use to indicate any other message."

"Five hundred and twenty bucks. Hmmm..."

"Yes sir. And because you advertised with us last year I can... throw in a hundred and fifty ink pens with your name and logo." Nervous beads of sweat popped up on her head.

"Well, people are always walking away with our pens... Alright Miss Michaels, you have yourself a deal."

Hayden had to resist jumping up on her desktop and doing the cabbage patch dance or the Icky Shuffle. She wasn't going to act like a novice by sounding all happy about it over the phone so she calmed herself and finished taking his information.

"I'll send the information right over to the printers and we will email you the proof. Thank you Mr. Lange."

After hanging up the phone Hayden leaned back in her chair and smiled. She jumped up and walked to the board where she placed her initials H.M. in the 5X9 area.

One hundred and fifty six bucks was hers. Now to sell another-

"Whoa, whoa, whoa!" Abdullah jumped to his feet and rushed to the board. He stared at it and then at Hayden with eyes ready to explode from his face.

"You stole my ad!" He yelled.

She gave him a surprised look. "What? I did not..." Her face burned in embarrassment when everyone's eyes moved to them. What was this crazy man talking about? She gestured to the board. "There is nothing written on the board-"

"But it's a re-run!"

Abdullah's face darkened in fury as the blood rushed to it. He was just her height and had thin black hair and a perpetually greasy sheen to his tanned face. His button down shirt was rolled up to his elbows and his collar was opened exposing a puff of black chest hair. He pointed an angry finger at her and for a moment Hayden thought he intended to hit her.

"Re-run?" she asked weakly. What in the hell was a re-run? "I-I'm sorry. I didn't know-"

He rolled his eyes and threw his hands into the air. "So now you're going to play innocent, and act like you didn't know?" His loud angry voice boomed through the room.

"Abdullah," came a sharp voice. "That's enough." They both turned and she expected to see Mr. Fox, but it was Brian/Brine. He was covering the mouthpiece of his phone and glaring at Abdullah, gesturing with his other hand for him to go away, back to his desk or out the door, but away from the work area. He quickly returned to his caller. "Yes, Mr. Stanley, I'm still here. Yes, sorry about that...uh..."

Abdullah raised his hands imploringly to all the onlookers, his anger not yet abated although he did lower his voice. "This always happens every time Fox hires another pretty girl. They prance in here thinking that just because they flash a big smile or bat their eyes while they are stealing your sale that you're supposed to just roll over and say, 'oh, it's okay.' No! I'm not going to be a fool and give up my commission!"

His dark eyes flashed at her again. "I don't care if you sold it or not, it's my commission and I'm taking it!" He then turned and stormed back to his desk, muttering under his breath.

Hayden didn't know what to say. She began to shake in a rage that was laced with embarrassment and outrage that some man would holler at her over a simple mistake. She wanted to tell him to take his little commission and shove it and then she wanted to run out the door, jump in her car and... wait... did he just call her pretty? *This happens every time Fox hires another pretty girl...* What in the hell? Was he blind?

Her heartbeat slowed as she contemplated the hidden meaning behind his words. Maybe he was just trying to soften the blow of his—no that wasn't it; he wasn't trying to soften anything. He was really pissed.

Hayden's own anger slowly began to diffuse, and she turned to go back to her desk. That was when she met Pam's eyes. The older woman quickly looked away, but not before Hayden saw the smug look on her face. Immediately, she knew that Pam had intentionally done this.

That was it! She was going to...

"Hey."

Her head swung over to Brian—or Brine, whatever his name was. His hand covered the mouthpiece of his phone, his brow still pulled into a deep frown. Crap, was he going to lay into her too? His customer had probably overheard the entire altercation, but it wasn't her fault if he lost his sale!

"Look, I didn't know about the re-runs-"

"Come over here. And bring your chair."

She hesitated. "Why?"

"So I can teach you how to sale vinyl." He then quickly moved his hand from the mouthpiece and continued talking to his customer in an animated, cheerful voice that didn't match the expression on his face. After another pause, Hayden got her chair and moved it in front of his desk.

Then she sat down and waited quietly for him to finish his call. He watched her as he talked to his customer. He sure did stare a lot. It unsettled her, or maybe it wasn't the staring as much as it was his big grey eyes that held an open expression. He was like a curious toddler taking in something new and interesting.

She returned his stare, hoping to teach him a lesson but it didn't appear to affect him. She allowed her eyes to roam his form, taking complete stock of him. He was too thin. She could see the sharp lines of his jaw with its after-five shadow.

He also seemed unnaturally pale, especially conspicuous because of the shadows beneath his eyes. Maybe he was getting over some type of illness. When he wasn't sickly-looking, he was probably quite handsome. He had thick blonde-brown hair that fell into his face threatening to disrupt his line of vision, but he didn't bother to move it aside. His fingers were drumming along his desk as he spoke, an almost nervous gesture, despite the calm, confident way that he spoke to his customer.

"Well Mr. Stanley, if you pay with a credit card I can knock another fifty dollars off the cost since I won't have to pay my man to come down to collect, fair enough? Alright sir, then I'll give you to Ginger who will get your credit card information. Hey, it was good doing business with you again. You have a good evening, too." He transferred the call and the smile that had been on his face while talking to his customer suddenly fell away.

"I'm sorry about that," he said.

She frowned. "About what?"

"Abdullah."

"Oh." She wondered why he was apologizing for Abdullah. "It's okay. I guess he didn't believe that I didn't know about re-runs."

His eyes flitted to Pam. Ah... so he probably suspected that she had done it on purpose, too. Maybe she always did this and Abdullah was always the one getting his sales stolen by the *pretty girls* that just happened to be poorly trained by Pam. The hateful heifer...

He got up and scribbled something on the board. As he did, his long thin body moved gracefully, despite the awkward angles of elbows and knees in loose fitting jeans and a long-sleeved polo shirt.

"You're *Brian*, right?" she asked when he was settled back behind his desk.

One brow flitted up at the emphasis that she put on his name. "Yes. And you're Hayden." His hands moved anxiously over the papers on his desk, meticulously straightening them as he spoke. "Have you ever done telemarketing before this?"

"No." She could have said that she was familiar with it because of her ex, but she didn't want to go there.

His brow flitted up again. "Well you have a very good voice for sales."

Her face warmed. She had never liked compliments... if that's what this was. "I do customer service at my first job. So I talk on the phone a lot."

He nodded. "Well the key to telemarketing is to convince the perspective buyer that they have a need and that *you* have what can satisfy that need. You don't say 'hey do you want to advertise on our phonebook cover?' You say, 'I see that you have a small business on the corner of something and other. If you can increase

34

your reach to more people in your community, then it would obviously increase your sales.'"

Hayden nodded in agreement.

"It becomes a no-brainer situation that only a dimwit would turn down, or at least that is what you will make them think."

Hayden watched him intently, remembering that MyKell used to always tell her how he made his customers basically admit that they were dumbasses for turning down what he was selling.

"The company distributes anywhere from twenty to forty thousand phonebook covers within the target city. Remember to say that; as well as ten complimentary covers going to the owner. *Then* you tell them the price."

Hayden wondered if he had been listening to her sales technique, and the idea of it slightly embarrassed her. She had strongly underestimated Telemarketers. There was a lot more to it than just reading a script.

Brian told her about trade-outs; deadbeats, and the bottom line price; what it cost to actually make the ad, including all over-head so that if she ever hit the bottom line price there would be no commission going to her. Then he explained when it would be in her favor to make a sale with no commission; for instance when there was bonus money for whoever closed their set first, or when there was a deadline that needed to be met because the cover couldn't go to the printers until every ad was sold. He emphasized that she was never ever to go below the bottom line price. Then he explained that once she made a sale it was always hers to call back each year as a re-run.

Hayden listened raptly to the information that Brian shared. "But if I have to wait for everyone else to call the re-runs I won't be left with anything-"

He shook his head. "Not many people work here long enough to collect years of reruns. There are only five on this set and we split the rest. Unfortunately, you grabbed the wrong one." He pointed to the clipboard with its mock up telephone cover. "Behind the cover is a list of who sold what in the prior year. You will see that the 5x9 is owned by Abdullah."

Hayden shook her head, feeling pretty low for not knowing something as simple as that.

"Hayden." She looked at him again. "It's not so bad. You sold that ad for more then Abdullah did last year. You made him full commission..." he leaned in and whispered, "something he obviously couldn't do, right?"

She smiled, liking Brian. It was cool of him to take the time to really teach her the important aspects of their job.

She gave him a curious look. "Why doesn't Mr. Fox let you train the new hires?" He obviously took more pride in it than Pam did.

He looked down at his desk and then just shook his head slightly. "I guess that's all," he finally said.

"Oh... Okay, thank you." She hoped that she hadn't said anything wrong.

With a brief nod, he stood and then left the room. Hayden watched him walk tiredly into the canteen, curious about why he'd taken the time to help her when he obviously hadn't been directed to do so by Mr. Fox. Also, why wasn't his knowledge being put to use by Mr. Fox?

She gathered her things and then went to the board to see which spaces were free for her to call. She scowled when she saw that Abdullah had scribbled out her initials and replaced them with his own. B.F. were the only other initials listed. Hayden was even more determined than ever to add her sale to the board before Pam's child-like drawing of a heart, which took the place of her initials. It was Hayden's goal in life to now out-do Pam in every way.

~Chapter 5~
THE STRIDES WE MAKE

Hayden fell into bed in near exhaustion. Clean cotton sheets enveloped her freshly showered body and a smile was frozen on her face even hours after she had drifted off to sleep. She had made her second sale and had done it before Pam had made even one. As far as she was concerned, all was right with the world.

The next morning Hayden stared at the calendar as the oatmeal that she cooked and refrigerated in small batches each weekend heated in the microwave. The night before, Hayden had written the newest affirmation on the monthly notes section of her calendar. Her writing had been almost like cat scratch in her fatigue, but at the time, it seemed very important to have it written so that she could read it this morning.

The way I treat people who I seek and expect nothing from is the same way I treat those I hope to gain and learn from.

Hayden stared at the words, repeating them, feeling them and then finally trying to accept them. She wouldn't mind being friends with Brian, but there was no way that she would reach out in a friendly way to Pam... or even to Abdullah. She retrieved her oatmeal in deep thought and then sat down to eat it.

The hell with that... she scowled. Yet as she rode the recumbent bike at the gym, Hayden couldn't stop thinking that the meaning of her latest affirmation was not quite so obvious. Friendship was based on trust and only a fool would trust a backstabbing she-dog!

She was back home and showering away the musk of her workout when she finally came to an understanding of the words that kept playing over and over again in her head. She was standing with her face turned to the spray of the water, feeling a calmness fill her as she reverted to a meditative state. It felt so good to feel her sore muscles being soothed by the hot spray. This calm was the way she wished to always feel.

Hayden's eyes suddenly popped open. So then why would she allow a person like Pam to affect her? Yesterday, she had almost lost her cool, until Brian called her over to his desk.

It was Pam's own sad fault that she was hateful. Besides, what did Hayden really care? That woman was so far beneath her that she didn't even enter her line of vision. There was just too much going on in Hayden's own life to waste even an ounce of energy playing get-back-at-Pam games.

Hayden smiled to herself, blinking her wet lashes. Yep, if a person doesn't negatively impact her, then it was nothing to treat them the way she would treat any other person, right? *That* was the real meaning behind the affirmation.

Hayden went through the remainder of her morning in high spirits despite the fact that it was Friday; the last day of a long, hard week and by all rights she should be utterly exhausted. She and Dani were hurrying back to work from a corner coffee shop where they had taken their last break. Dani was sipping from an obnoxiously large, whipped cream-laden concoction and Hayden grimaced when she thought about the amount of calories in just that one drink—probably more than she herself would consume in a whole day.

Yet Dani's voluptuous body was cute and bounced and moved in all the right ways so she was content with her weight. "Hayden, I'm telling you that this guy is gorgeous, funny, has a good job—seriously, you should meet him."

Hayden resisted the urge to roll her eyes. Dani kept bringing up this guy that was friends with her boyfriend. He was supposed to be tall, dark, handsome *and* single.

He had no children and... he was single. He was funny and... guess what else? He was single. Dani seemed to think that she needed to fall into line and quickly snatch him up before some other woman did. Dani didn't seem to understand that a love interest was the last thing on Hayden's mind — as if her ego could stand rejection from two men in the same year.

Hayden shook her head adamantly. "Nope. Not going to happen."

"What are you waiting for? You lost like twenty pounds and you're looking great. Plus it's been over two months since... well, MyKell left. It helps to have someone when you're getting over someone else, Hayden."

Hayden cringed at the sound of *his* name being spoken out into the air. "This is a horrible time to meet someone. I'm really super busy-"

"Yes you are! All you do is work and exercise. I mean I know it's therapeutic, but not if you're using it as a way to hide!"

Hayden sighed regretting that she hadn't told her best friend about her plans to disregard this entire year as just a huge stepping-stone to betterment. Then Dani would understand that there was nothing but self-improvement happening until she reached her goal. Deep down, Hayden understood that it wasn't healthy to completely detach herself from her own life. Yet, because of this decision, she had never once cheated on her diet or ended her workout even one minute before she was supposed to.

Had she tried doing this any other way then she would have already failed. If she failed... well there was just no reason to be. She would forever be that person that said she would lose weight; that made the New Year's resolutions, that paid good money for the diets, but who never followed through.

So if she couldn't find some sense of self-pride, then the woman that she had turned into would always disgust her. This throwaway year actually gave her life a purpose. It was penance, reward and self-discovery, and failure was not an option!

Hayden took a deep breath and met her friend's eyes. "I will meet this man, but only when I've met my personal goal. Not one moment before."

Dani smiled. "That's all I want. We should go shopping this weekend. Your clothes are too big."

"What?" Dani was really dropping the subject that easily? Hayden cringed again. "No shopping. I still have a long way to go before I spend money on clothes."

"Uh... then it's time for you to start digging through your old clothes for the smaller sizes. Because pretty soon, your pants are going to fall down right around your ankles!"

Hayden patted the belt that was cinched around her waist and hidden by her blouse. She knew that the material was bunched together and hoped that it wasn't too noticeable. Obviously it was. Well being unsightly was not in the plans! So this weekend she would make the time to go down into the basement and dig through the plastic containers full of her old clothes.

Hmmm. Maybe Dani was right. Hayden should spend some money on some new outfits. After all, she was going to need running shoes if she was going to do the Zombie Run. Yep... it was time to go shopping.

"Alright, Saturday we're hitting the mall," Hayden finally conceded.

Dani beamed and gave her a side-look as if she had something up her sleeves.

Hayden narrowed her eyes. "I mean it Dani. I'm not meeting that guy until I'm ready."

"No, that's fine! I'm just happy we're going to hang out this weekend."

By the time Hayden made it to Fox Vinyl, the fatigue of a long, difficult week finally hit her. She tried to suppress her yawns but her day began at 5:00 A.M. every single weekday and didn't end until 11:00 P.M. The only thing that got her going each morning was the fact that her daily workout gave her energy and woke her better than a strong cup of coffee. However, that energy was long gone by now.

When she arrived in the evenings everyone else on her team would already be present – not counting breaks to the canteen – since they worked a full shift to her part-time hours. The first thing she did as she headed to her desk tonight was to check the board for the number of sales. Brian and Marcus each had two, Abdullah had four, and there was one each for her and Pam. Only two for Brian? He usually led the team in sales.

She looked over at his desk and saw that it was empty. It appeared that he hadn't been in all day. Well she hoped that he took the weekend to get some rest and to get over his illness. The last thing she needed was to catch someone's germs and to end up sick and flat on her back.

Hayden sat down and got her materials together and then she looked over at Abdullah. He was scanning the phonebook, his finger scrolling down the page and his mouth moving as he read to himself. *The way I treat people who I seek and expect nothing from is the same way I treat those I hope to gain and learn from...*

Taking a deep breath, she stood and trudged across the aisle to his desk. He looked at her without changing his posture.

"Abdullah, I just wanted to apologize again about yesterday. And I hope that..." *what do I hope? I didn't want to be friends and I am not about to lie about it.* "...we can put that behind us."

The ensuing silence dragged on. *Okay...* When he didn't move she made to turn, but then, he nodded slowly.

"I'm sorry as well. I should not have yelled at you. I had no right."

She was surprised by his apology, but she simply nodded and then returned to her seat with a smile. That had felt good. Pam returned to her desk a few minutes later from her smoke break in the canteen. Hayden couldn't force herself to speak to that one and decided that the next best thing was to just disregard her.

A little later, Marcus, or Mr. Doo Wop, asked her if she wanted a cup of coffee after he walked past and saw her mouth wide open in a deep yawn. With embarrassment, she explained that she no longer drank coffee. Equally important was that she wouldn't dare eat or drink anything that had come from that dirty canteen, but she kept that little tidbit to herself.

"You let me know if you need something to perk you up," he whispered before walking back to his desk.

Hayden froze. Did he just offer her drugs... or something sexual? Ugh... he was her daddy's age! Double ugh, as if she would take unknown drugs from some stranger! She tried to wipe the yuck-look from her face as she returned to her work feeling slightly traumatized.

Four hours moved by quickly and by the end of the evening she had another sale. Woot! Woot! She wasted no time leaving work. Then after her shower, she fell into bed naked, and was deeply asleep right on top of her neatly made bed.

For once in a very long time, Hayden found clothes' shopping was actually enjoyable. When she picked out slacks to try on, she found that they were way too big and she had to send Dani running around the store for smaller and then even smaller sizes. Then when she stepped out of the dressing room wearing pants that actually hugged her legs and butt and, they looked so good that she was in awe.

She had wanted simple blouses, but Dani convinced her to find pretty shirts that accentuated a waistline that she hadn't had in ages. Now she could see that Dani was right. The prettier blouses, the better fitting clothes... made her feel pretty.

"I told you!" Dani was standing beside her as she looked in the large mirror that stood at the entrance of the dressing room. Hayden looked at the reflection of her and her best friend standing side-by-side.

She was smaller than Dani, but... Hayden allowed her eyes to move to Dani's face and then to her own. Wide brown eyes stared back at her from a golden brown face that could no longer be called round. Neat twirls from her teeny weeny afro haloed her head. She didn't have a pig face at all...

Her eyes scanned her entire form. No, she wasn't thin, but she was far from being the fat girl that she had been in her mind's eye. So why was it that when she took off her clothes, she still saw nothing but rolls of ugly fat?

Hayden did a slight turn and checked out her side view. Wow, was that her butt? When had it lifted like that, when it had always been wide and flat before?

Dani was smiling at her in the mirror. "See? You look good."

Hayden blushed and looked away and then she headed back to the dressing room to change, but while she did she had a smile on her face. She glanced down at her body in just panties and a bra. Yeah, that extra roll on each side of her body was gone now... she was down to just one. There was still work to be done, but she really had made great strides.

~Chapter 6~
THE LOSS OF PROGRESS = A FRESH START

Hayden spent the weekend sorting through her old clothes and she actually got rid of any sizes that were now too big for her. She would never allow herself to get that big again, and if she did, then she would just have to bear the consequences of having to buy an entirely new wardrobe. Two garbage bags of clothes went into her trunk to be donated to the nearby Good Will.

On Sunday, she and Todd began their first day of marathon training. He had sent her a text instructing her to meet him at the entrance of Sharon Woods Park. She arrived timely at 9:00 A.M. and parked her car next to Todd's truck.

He got out of his truck and was about to greet her when he took a double take. She was wearing shorts. Shorts! She had on a t-shirt that hugged her body instead of her normally oversized ones that fell over her butt. Her new $60 sneakers donned her feet.

"Hi Hayden. *So…* you're looking good." He was wearing a cheesy grin. "You finally figured it out."

She rolled her eye. "Thank you." She tried not to blush and wondered if people would think that they were a couple…

Sharon Woods had a great jogging trail that Todd liked. Hayden had been to the park many times, but had never ventured onto the trail. It wove through the forest on dirt paths across a wooden bridge and alongside a rocky creek. She had no idea that there was so much beauty in this park. Todd didn't make her run or jog but he did insist that she maintain a fast walk. Other joggers passed them, and she saw people who were there just to walk and enjoy the scenery or to toss rocks into the creek.

"This place is so beautiful. I can't believe I've never been to this part of the park before."

"Kia and I brought the boys here yesterday." He pointed ahead to a signpost that described the dinosaurs that had roamed the area. "Kevin, who is ten, did a hurdle over that post."

"Are you serious? That thing's over four feet high."

"I think he's going to be a runner." Todd smiled. "He wants to do the Zombie run with me."

"Then you should bring him along to train with us," she offered. School was out and she liked the stories that he told about Kia and the boys. His wife seemed really down to earth and the boys obviously loved Todd just like he loved them.

He squinted at her. "You sure you wouldn't mind? You do pay me to focus my training on you."

"Well, I'm hoping that he'll run slower than me."

Todd chuckled. "So, I'll do this; when we're out of the gym there is no charge for the training."

"But-"

"Since I have to train too, and if Kevin is coming along, then we should just consider it a training partnership."

"Hell yeah! You got a deal!" A dollar saved, was a dollar earned!

When they finally returned to their cars, Hayden was tired. If she was this tired from just an hour of fast walking, how was she going to handle an hour of running? Todd stated that he would see her at the gym Tuesday and instructed her to begin walking the treadmill again.

"I want your pace as fast as we were walking today, okay?"

"Got it."

"No running yet. I'm going to start you on intervals of thirty-seconds. Walk for three minutes and then fast run for thirty seconds." She nodded, hoping that she wouldn't look totally stupid when she fell off the treadmill, which was sure to happen. *YouTube, here I come…*

Yet by Monday, Hayden felt in high spirits. She was actually looking forward to her second job as she began looking at her

45

sales as a test of her abilities and not just getting to the money. Marcus winked at her as she took her seat and Hayden gave him a quick wave and then averted her eyes in case he tried to flirt or offer her drugs again.

Brian had returned, but he didn't look much better. He wore a somber expression and seemed distracted. He didn't even stare today. However, he did say hello when he passed her desk on the way to the canteen for his break. He even congratulated her on her new sales.

Mr. Fox came out of his office to tell her how well she was performing and Pam nearly broke her neck to agree that she was doing extremely well—somehow syphoning the credit onto herself.

"I had some very good help," Hayden responded simply.

"Well, you keep it up. Next week we're going to have a monthly bonus. It's a thousand dollars. Top seller wins."

Now that was some good motivation. Not that she thought she could outsell all of the experienced Telemarketers, but it would be nice to outsell some of them.

Mr. Fox headed back to his office and looked at Brian's desk. "Where is he?" his voice was suddenly very nasty.

Hayden looked at him in surprise and Pam quickly answered. "He's taking a smoke."

Mr. Fox grunted in displeasure and then returned to his office.

Brian was only gone ten minutes and when he returned Pam spoke to him in her fake saccharin voice. "Brine, he was looking for you."

Hayden noticed the look that crossed his face. Was Brian afraid of Mr. Fox? He nodded and then quickly returned to work.

At the end of the evening, Hayden was happy to see that she had twice as many sales as Pam—who seemed to take it as a personal attack every time Hayden got up to write her initials on the board. One sale a day might not get Hayden a thousand bucks, but in a four-hour shift, it wasn't too shabby. At the end of the shift, she didn't immediately dart out the door like she normally did either.

She made sure that her order forms were correct for the printers because she had seen how Pam spent so much time talking to customers about mistakes on the layout. As she was heading out the door, she heard a loud noise from Mr. Fox's office; as if someone had thrown or slammed something, and then his muffled voice cursing up a blue streak. At first she thought that he might have fallen until she understood that his words were directed at someone.

She could only make out a few of them but she clearly heard the repeated use of the word *fuck* as in, "fuck-up," "where the fuck," and "who the fuck."

Marcus was walking out the door whistling and doing a pimp walk. He didn't even seem to notice or care that Mr. Fox was going off on someone. She lagged behind until the office door swung open and Brian came walking out. Mr. Fox was still yelling at him.

"You don't have that many more chances here! Do you hear me?"

Brian looked over his shoulder back into the office. "I was sick!"

"Well that's your fault, not mine!"

Brian walked away, his face an angry mask. Hayden hurried out the door. Damn, she was never going to call in sick…

On Tuesday, Hayden had interval training with Todd at the gym. While she did not fall off the treadmill, she did beg him with her eyes to allow her to stop before her lungs flew out of her mouth. However, he had no mercy. He kept his hand on the speed button moving it up when it was time for her to sprint and then back to a medium walk for the next three minutes. He made her keep doing those intervals for an entire half an hour!

At the end, she didn't speak; she just stumbled to the lockers where she puked up her morning oatmeal into the toilet. When she walked back into the main area of the gym, Todd was waiting for her with bottled water. She never bought the bottled water when there was a water faucet that she could use for free, but she took the peace offering while he watched her meekly.

"Are you okay?"

She nodded. "I got sick, but yeah, I'm okay."

"It's your breathing; you're going to have to learn to regulate it. You have to find your second wind."

She huffed. "It didn't seem like it wanted to be found." She knew what he was talking about. When she rode the bike, there was a point at about fifteen minutes in when she thought that she would keel over and die, but if she pushed on it would suddenly get easier and her legs would begin pedaling madly until she hit the wall and found her *third* wind.

Later, as Hayden's day moved on, it seemed to go from bad to worse. She was late getting to work because she made the mistake of going through the drive through at McDonald's for more oatmeal. Unfortunately, the line was slow and long. She ended up being ten minutes late to work and by the time she had a chance to eat; the oatmeal was a cold, hard lump that she dumped into her trashcan.

Then by the time lunch came, she was starving but had packed only a chef salad, not even half a sandwich or a fruit cup to go along with it. She was staring into her empty bowl wishing for seconds when Dani invited her to the Jazz Festival. The Jazz Festival was a big deal in her city.

The top R&B singers and groups were sure to appear. Then of course, there would be the old-time groups that never went out of style like Frankie Beverly and Maze and Patti Labelle. It was something that she and MyKell had attended every summer.

Hayden's life had been running smoothly not counting the week directly following her breakup with MyKell when she'd had her meltdown. Beyond that, she had coped with the end of a six-year relationship with as much detachment as she could muster.

Yet every bit of ground that she had gained in the last two months was thrown out the window at the mention of the Jazz Festival. The realization that she would never go to the Jazz Festival with MyKell again first stunned, and then hurt her so deeply that it was like being bowled over.

MyKell would go to the Jazz Festival with someone else... It was over. He wasn't coming back. He was no longer a part of her life.

Hayden could have clutched her chest as the pain of it sank in for her. The sudden grief brought swift stinging tears to her eyes and she could no longer speak. All she could do was look away and shake her head, praying that the tears filling her eyes didn't fall.

Dani gasped. "Oh Hayden, I'm sorry. I didn't mean to... I just want you to have fun. You're so much better off without that asshole! Don't you know how much he used you for your kindness? So he moved on to some other woman that he can use up. Good riddance!"

Oh my God... Hayden didn't want to have this conversation. Not when the tears were welling up in her eyes and they were sitting in the break room with their co-workers. However, Hayden had lost the ability to use her voice and didn't know how to tell her friend to stop. Just stop...

"Look, Hayden, if you change your mind just let me know, okay?" Dani touched her hand and Hayden just nodded her head. Dani quickly changed the subject and Hayden was grateful that a moment later her tears receded.

After their lunch break, Hayden went back to her desk, too afraid that if she stopped at the restroom the tears would return. She stared at her computer screen hands slack in her lap. *There is no joy in my life. This is all...*

Hayden had stopped at McDonald's again on her way to Fox Vinyl. She ordered a large chocolate shake, a double quarter pounder with cheese and a super sized order of fries with two apple pies. Her stomach ached terribly by the time that she entered the building.

Not because she had eaten all of that fast food, but because she had thrown it out the window and now her stomach felt like an empty cavern. She never packed an evening meal because she wouldn't have time to spare reheating a packed meal for dinner when she had one hour from the end of one job and the beginning of the next. So there was no way that she could survive on sandwiches and salads all week long for each of her three meals. Dinner was the time that she splurged on carryout; either a roast chicken dinner from Boston Market, or Italian Wedding Soup from the deli, and if she was lucky, the roast turkey special from The Cracker Barrel.

She'd blown that though…

Hayden walked into the little canteen for the first time since being an employee of Fox Vinyl, her stomach making sounds that unnerved her. It was worse than she had imagined. No surprise that the ashtrays and trashcans were overflowing but the floor was sticky. She didn't have to open the microwave to see that it was totally filthy… she could smell it! It smelled like… Abdullah.

The tables appeared to have been cleaned with a dirty sponge. She couldn't even smell the Pine Sol that she had used on all of the surfaces when she was the cleaning lady. Did the new person even use disinfectant?

Hayden couldn't hide the grimace on her face as she headed for the vending machines. She carefully studied the contents but there was absolutely nothing even remotely healthy inside of any of them. She finally settled on two cartons of orange juice. She would have gone for a carton of skim milk but couldn't see the expiration date and something told her that she really shouldn't trust the milk in the vending machine.

She was about to leave when she saw Brian waving at her from a table where he sat alone smoking a cigarette. She waved back and he gestured for her to come over. Well, why not? She never took breaks and everyone else got up at least once an hour.

Mr. Fox didn't seem to have a policy concerning breaks — evidenced by the amount that Pam took.

"Hey Hayden."

She sat down across from him. "Hi Brian, how's it going?"

"Pretty good." He picked up his pack of cigarettes and offered her one.

She shook her head. "No thank you. I don't smoke."

He took a last puff and then smashed it into the ashtray, turning his head to blow the smoke away from her. She opened one of the cartons of OJ and downed it hungrily. Her stomach groaned loudly and Brian gave her a shocked look.

"Oh, I'm sorry! That was just my stomach!"

He smiled in amusement. "Yeah, you're hungry."

She shrugged but was happy to see him smiling. He always appeared so somber, and when he smiled it changed his face completely. He was too pale, too thin, but suddenly he was also kind of cute.

"I didn't have time for dinner," she explained.

"Orange juice for dinner?"

"Well... I'm trying to eat healthy. So..."

"Ah. Right. There is nothing healthy to be found in this room."

She opened the second carton but was a bit more ladylike as she took a small swallow. "I hear there's going to be a big bonus in a few weeks. A thousand bucks," she said.

"They do it every month, or something close to it."

"I bet you've won it a few times."

He smiled and looked down. "No. I've only been doing sales for a few weeks."

She frowned at him, not believing what he was telling her. He knew too much about everything.

He noticed her look. "Well, I've been with Fox for years but not telemarketing. I delivered the phonebook covers and..." his voice softened. "Sometimes I'd pick up the money from the customers or just... whatever needed to be done."

She was curious about Mr. Fox and why he came down so hard on Brian. However, Hayden had no intention of being nosey.

"Do you like working here?"

His eyes flitted away before settling back on her.

"Not really." He looked at the clock above the door. "I better get back."

"Yeah, me too."

She followed him back to the work area, checking the board for sales as she headed to her desk. She slumped down into her chair and was trying to concentrate on the phonebook when she caught a movement in front of her desk. She looked up in time to see Brian heading back across the aisle to his own desk. She looked at him curiously before noticing that there was a big golden delicious apple on the corner of her desk sitting on top of her inbox.

A smile tugged at her lips and when Brian sat down and looked at her she mouthed, "thank you." He nodded and put the remainder of his bag lunch in one of his desk drawers. She picked up the apple and rubbed it on her pants before taking a big bite. She decided that she liked working at Fox Vinyl.

Long after the apple was eaten, Hayden's head was buried in the phonebook and she was lost in thought. Unfortunately, they weren't work related thoughts. She hadn't made a sale all night and she only had an hour left on her shift. She just couldn't seem to get it together. Instead of seeing the businesses listed on the pages, she kept thinking thoughts that were best left buried.

Like, what did that other woman look like; the one that MyKell preferred over her? Did he miss Hayden at all? Did he even think about her?

She was struggling with these thoughts when she felt someone standing in front of her desk. She looked up to the sight of Marcus. He was smiling at her.

"I was just checking that you hadn't fallen asleep sitting there. You've been looking at that same page for five minutes."

How would he know unless he was watching her for five minutes? She offered him a weak smile and then returned to the phonebook, making a point to turn the page. When he didn't leave she looked up again.

He leaned down and spoke in a semi-low voice. "Look, I don't mean any disrespect but you look very down and if you need a pick me up, you just let me know. I have pills or weed or whatever, okay?"

"Oh." Her eyes widened. "Okay…"

He winked and walked away.

Her brow furrowed. Good God, what was she going to do about this man trying to push drugs on her? She didn't want to have to deal with this every freaking day, especially with everything else that she was dealing with. She closed her eyes and tried to think of one of the affirmations that she had saved on her laptop, but she could not bring even one of them to mind.

~Chapter7~
PERFECTLY IMPERFECT

Hayden had given into her tears as she lay curled in bed later that night, calling them for what they were; tears of loneliness and shame. She was ashamed that she still loved MyKell and disgusted that she wanted him to beg her for forgiveness. She would forgive him too because living with her weakness was far better than the feeling of rejection that lay curdling inside of her belly.

She blinked her eyes and sat up in bed. No, that wasn't really true. She would *not* take MyKell Juarez back. She sat frozen as she analyzed and found that to be a definitive fact.

If he even put his hands on her now, she would hurl and the idea of him inside of her body was beyond disgusting. Hayden's heart leapt in excitement as she realized that this was the truest feeling that she had experienced all day. She turned on her lamp as she counted all of the things that she despised about her ex. The list was much longer than the things that she liked about him.

She huffed, and wiped the tears from her cheeks. He was a cheap man who had no problems having her take care of him. Him finding someone else was probably a blessing because now he was someone else's problem. Besides, she hadn't felt any sense of respect for the man in years. She couldn't even pinpoint the exact moment that she had stopped taking pride in him and had internalized her dislike of him.

Oh my God... she didn't like MyKell and hadn't liked him in years. Hayden cradled her face in her hands. *Things hadn't been right for a long time...* MyKell knew it and now she could admit it too.

Hayden jumped out of bed, not even sure what time it was, only knowing that it was late and that she should be asleep. Yet she wouldn't be able to do that until she got on her laptop and found something that she had read in her list of affirmations. In this moment of her life, there was nothing truer than those words…

When she found it, she read the words over and over until she had it burned into her memory. Perhaps this was her motto. It definitely was not a momentary inspiration, but rather, a lifetime lesson.

Hayden closed her laptop and then returned to bed a much calmer woman. When she drifted into a peaceful sleep a short time later, it was carried on the wings of a dream that included a golden delicious apple. The next morning Hayden wrote her newest affirmation in black magic marker across the top of her calendar instead of in the usual note area in back.

I am perfectly imperfect. I strive for better while loving all that I am today. In loving myself today, I am better equipped to improve myself tomorrow.

Hayden smiled and nodded and then headed for the gym. Today she would do the intervals even though Todd hadn't told her to. She knew that she could do it because if she set her mind to it, she could do anything.

When Hayden walked to her desk at her second job, she saw that the board was empty and that there was a new phonebook sitting there. Again she was excited and motivated to make a fresh start in a new book. She greeted Brian with a quick wave and he tilted his head in acknowledgment. Then she looked over at Abdullah and when he met her eyes, she gave him a silent greeting mimicking the head move that Brian had given her.

Abdullah gave the head move back and although she didn't want to open the lines of communication with Marcus, she did the same thing to him, which he returned with a flourished bow and wink. Pam wouldn't even look in her direction, so she did not receive a greeting at all. By the end of the night, Hayden had two sales! She decided that she liked the city of Springfield, Illinois.

When Brian went up to the board to add his initials, he gave Hayden an impressed look.

"High five Hayden!" He raised his hand at her and she wasn't sure if she was supposed to high five back or just laugh at him. White people were the only ones who still did high fives. She smacked his hand.

"Thanks for that apple yesterday. It hit the spot."

"Well you're looking less hungry. I mean… uh, I didn't mean anything by that," he stammered appearing flustered.

"It's okay." She knew that she was overweight and had never been easily offended over it. Perhaps she should have cared more and then she wouldn't be throwing away an entire year to get herself together.

They were chatting about the Springfield area when Pam abruptly cleared her throat. They looked over and saw that Mr. Fox was heading for them. Brian stared at him while Hayden moved to her phonebook and began speaking loudly.

"Thank you Brian. I understand now. You have been so helpful and have made it so easy to understand." Okay, so maybe she was overdoing it, but she wanted Mr. Fox to know that Brian was helping her to be a better salesperson.

"Hello Hayden," he said.

"Hi Mr. Fox."

The man's attention turned to Brian. "I need to see you in my office," and then he abruptly turned away.

Brian didn't immediately follow, but Hayden saw his body stiffen as if in resolve. He raised his brow at her and gave her a crooked smile.

"The boss calls," and then he disappeared into Mr. Fox's office.

At the end of her shift, Hayden knew that she shouldn't linger but Brian was still in Mr. Fox's office and it was pissing her off even though she didn't hear any yelling. Still, the man was taking him from his calls—causing him to be unproductive. It was obvious that Brian didn't enjoy working for his company. She decided that she would be nosey. In fact, she intended to be very nosey.

She waited outside in front of the plate glass door pretending to dig through her purse but peeking inside for any sight of Brian or Mr. Fox. Marcus came out and gave her a goodbye salute.

"Hey Marcus!"

"Yes young lady? How may I assist you?" he asked in a mock-baritone voice.

"Can I ask you something?" She gestured for him to follow her a few steps from the entrance so they wouldn't be overheard.

"Sure. What's up?" He had stopped clowning and was giving her a serious look now.

The door swung open and Brian came out. When he saw Hayden and Marcus he did a double take and then nodded in their direction before walking quickly to his vehicle.

A moment later, Mr. Fox came out. He waved at them.

"Goodnight you two."

"Have a good evening," Marcus called back and then gave Hayden a knowing look.

Oh damn! Now Marcus probably thought she wanted to purchase drugs from him. Well she would just have to settle that situation as well.

When the coast was clear, she looked at Marcus again. "I was curious about something. What's the deal between Mr. Fox and Brian?"

Marcus just looked at her in confusion as if the meaning of her words had escaped him. "What do you mean?"

"Well Mr. Fox is kind of an asshole. He yells at Brian-"

"Fox is the asshole?" Marcus' brow shot up. "No baby girl, Brian is the asshole."

Brian? What was he talking about? Brian didn't cut up, he didn't have an ego, and he was polite to everyone. Marcus placed a hand on her shoulder and she glanced at it in displeasure but didn't otherwise react.

"Let me explain something. Brian is an addict. I mean, I know that I come in here high as shit but that's weed or some pills. Hell, if I didn't come in here high I would go the fuck off on one of these silly mother fuckers over the phone." He chuckled and leaned in and spoke in a conspiratory tone. "And to be honest, I have told a few of these hillbillies to go to hell."

Hayden just stared at him.

"Yeah, well I don't mess with heroin... I might sniff some coke, but I don't shoot up. Anyway, Brian got himself hooked on heroin and shit started turning up missing. Phonebook covers weren't been distributed but he acted like he was delivering that shit. Then customers started complaining, threatening to sue because they were paying to advertise on vinyl that wasn't going further than the ten copies being sent to the buyer!

"So when Fox looked into it, he found out that Brian was doing hella shit like collecting money but saying the customer had 'dead-beated.' That's mail fraud and when you get into mail and wire fraud that kind of thing brings mandatory prison sentences. Federal prison, which ain't no joke."

"Wait a minute, Marcus," Hayden said in disbelief. "Why would Mr. Fox keep a drug addict and thief around?"

Marcus gave her a surprised look. "Brian *Fox*. Uh, you didn't know that he's the boss' son?"

After a stunned moment, Hayden simply shook her head.

Marcus pulled out a cigarette and lit up. "Well, there was a big trial over it and it practically wiped out Fox Vinyl. The only reason that Brian didn't go to jail is because of burden of proof. Fox didn't have to prove that he distributed thirty-thousand covers... they had to prove that he didn't."

Hayden was shaking her head, still staring at Marcus as if he had just told her that a cow was seen jumping over the moon.

"But Marcus... why would Mr. Fox let him come back here? I mean-"

"Because Fox is a good guy; a stupid guy, but a good guy. I would have kicked that spoiled little mother fucker's ass. You don't steal from your own father. You don't shit where you eat."

Hayden's nose wrinkled at his choice of words.

"Brian went to rehab." Marcus laughed. "Do you know anybody that's ever gone to rehab and stayed clean? Rehab is a fucking joke. You do it when you get busted and as soon as you get out, you're right back shooting, or huffing or snorting.

"Fox makes him pee in a cup. He said the first time it comes back dirty he's going to cut the kid off—permanently this time. No money. No Fox Vinyl to run when the old man dies. Nothing."

Hayden shook her head sadly. "I had no idea."

Marcus gave her a look as if she was pretty dumb. "You don't know what a heroin addict looks like? Why do you think Brian wears long-sleeved shirts in summer? Fox don't keep it that cool in here!"

Hayden ran her hand though her hair. "Uh Marcus, thanks for the information. I better head out. See you tomorrow." She turned for her car.

"Hey! You know if you need anything, just let me know."

Hayden stopped walking and turned around. "Marcus, I understand. You've made it really clear, okay?"

He chuckled. "Yeah. See you tomorrow baby girl." He began whistling as he headed for his own car.

Hayden felt horrible at the information that she'd just learned. Brian was a heroin addict who had stolen from his father. Damn, she was a great judge of character.

~Chapter 8~
HOW TO TREAT A FRIEND

Early Saturday morning, Hayden arrived at Sharon Woods Park before Todd. He had warned her that today they would jog and she was both anxious and nervous. Other than what she did on the treadmill, Hayden had not run since she'd been a child. Images of twisted ankles and falling on her face filled her mind.

His son was coming along and hopefully it would take some of the focus off her. Hayden got out of her car when Todd's truck pulled up alongside of her car. He was apologizing.

"Sorry we're late. Somebody thought they were going out in public with their pants sagging."

Hayden stared at the boy that sheepishly stepped from the passenger side of the truck. He was Black. Todd's son was Black? Hayden quickly wiped the surprised look from her face and greeted the boy.

"Hi Kevin. Nice to meet you."

"Kevin this is Miss Michaels."

"Hi Miss Michaels," came his polite response.

Todd put his arm on the boy's shoulder and it was obvious that Kevin enjoyed the attention. He was cute, probably ten or eleven and was dressed in cargo shorts and a South Park t-shirt.

"Okay, we're going to warm up with five minutes of fast walking and then we'll start a slow jog. Are we ready team?" He clapped his hands and Kevin nodded enthusiastically.

"I'm ready to run," Kevin announced. "I don't need to walk."

Todd shook his head as they headed across the street to the trail. "No, Kev. Didn't anybody ever tell you that you have to walk before you run?"

Kevin looked at him suspiciously. "No."

"Well, you do."

Hayden took in their interaction. So Todd's wife was African-American? He had never even hinted to it! She found it very telling that Todd didn't even think in terms of his family's color enough to even mention it casually. If it was possible, she found that she liked Todd even more now...

It turned out that there was something about jogging that was comfortable and rhythmic. Hayden didn't discover this until she had hit the proverbial 'wall' and was seeking her second wind. Kevin ran like a kid with boundless energy. Todd jogged as if he was just walking. Yet for Hayden, jogging wasn't as much running as it was stumbling, panting and gripping the sharp knife-like pain in her side.

When she thought that she would have to give up and lay down in the dirt, Hayden's lungs suddenly opened. She gulped air into her starving lungs and as dopamine began to flood her system, she felt herself moving a bit faster and smoother. When she caught up with Todd he looked at her with approval. They jogged at a steady pace until they reached a hill that finally stopped her. She planted her hands on her legs and tried to catch her breath.

Todd jogged back to her. "Keep walking or you'll stiffen." She did as he advised and a moment later began jogging again; albeit much slower, but this time she didn't stop until she reached the top of the hill.

Both Todd and Kevin were waiting for her at the top and when she finally reached them they applauded. She turned around and looked at how far she had come. She had come a very long way.

Hayden was still walking with a limp when Monday rolled around. Todd had instructed her to do a slow jog at each workout. Her entire body was sore and she even had sore muscles in her shins! She didn't even know that there were muscles in her shins.

By the time that she arrived at Fox Vinyl, she wasn't even excited that they had started a new book and that it was the first day for the bonus contest. Brian met her eyes as she headed to her desk and she nodded her head at him in greeting and then quickly looked away. Ever since she had found out that information about him, she hadn't wanted to get too friendly. She knew druggies from being a teenager and they wore everyone out, constantly needing to borrow money if they weren't stealing it or otherwise acting weird.

Each evening she did greet him, but she avoided meeting his eyes and if it appeared that he would talk to her, she pretended to be busy, or would begin making a phone call. There were some positive things to develop over the next few days though. Marcus had ceased his constant offers to be her pusher. Also, she figured out that Abdullah didn't smell funny. He just smelled like curry; the curry that he heated in the microwave each evening without bothering to cover it with a napkin.

Strangest of all was that one evening, as the day was rounding down to a close, Pam turned in her chair and spoke to her.

"You can't call transmission companies."

"What?" Hayden had heard Pam, but she just couldn't believe that Pam had initiated any communication with her.

"You can only advertise one type of company on the cover."

She stared at Pam wanting to tell her that she already knew that—no thanks to her.

"Well transmission falls under G for garage, or A for automotive," Pam continued.

Hayden didn't speak. Okay maybe she was right because that re-run of Abdullah's that she'd sold was an auto body business. She glanced at Brian to see if that was correct information, but he wasn't paying attention.

Pam continued. "So the guys are calling the first half of the book and anything that is automotive or garage is theirs to call. We get the back half and even though T falls in our territory, transmission wouldn't because it's still an activity that falls under what a garage or automotive would do. So we can't call transmission."

Okay that did make sense. Hayden nodded in appreciation at the information. "Thanks," she said briefly.

Pam just stared at her.

Hayden turned in her seat until Pam was facing her back. It was probably rude, but she didn't care. Pam probably wasn't being as helpful as she was just happy to find something Hayden was doing wrong.

Mr. Fox came over a few moments later and gestured for Brian to follow him. He did it every few days and Hayden assumed it was for a drug test. She couldn't help but to notice the way Brian seemed to sink. However, he got up and followed his father back into his office where the door was soundly shut.

Pam immediately jumped up and hurried to Hayden's desk.

"You stopped being friends with Brine."

Hayden looked at her in surprise. She couldn't believe that this hypocritical she-dog was in her business.

"What are you talking about? I haven't stopped anything. And besides, why do you care?"

Pam wouldn't meet her eyes. "Because I remember..." The older woman sighed and shook her head and then returned to her desk.

Hayden stabbed out the number of her next customer into her telephone, but right before it began to ring she hung it up and turned her chair to face Pam.

"What is it that you remember?"

Pam took a long time to acknowledge the question but Hayden waited. She finally sighed again. "I need a cigarette." She met Hayden's eyes. "Care to join me?"

In the filthy, smelly, foul canteen the two women found a table away from others who had come in to chat, smoke or eat. Mr. Fox didn't allow the smokers to congregate outside the building. He said it gave a bad impression. Considering the majority of the people that worked at Fox Vinyl, it would definitely appear that a 12-step program was being held here if they were to gather outside...

Pam lit a cigarette, which she retrieved from a large coin purse. After she had taken a few puffs, she looked at Hayden.

"Me and Brine's mama were friends." She coughed into her hand and Hayden grimaced at the idea of all of the surfaces she would touch with that hand.

"We had worked together down in Dillard at a shipping company and when I came up here years later, I saw that she had married Robert and had Brine. Evidently it took them a long time to have him. That's why they treated him so special. Some might describe it as spoiling him, but I don't agree. He was special because of how hard it was to get him, that's all.

"Anyway, I didn't care too much for my job. I was working customer service at a collection agency and Brine's mama told me about this new company that Robert was trying to start." Pam shrugged. "So I started working here. I'd see Brine about once or twice a week. He was ten or eleven and his Daddy would tell him that he had to learn the business because one day, it was going to be his."

Pam smiled to herself. "Brine always looked around like this place was more than a rented office space where people down on their luck tried to sale ad space on phonebook covers. Robert would sit him with me so I could teach him how to be a telemarketer and Brine actually made sales, even as a kid. He wouldn't take none of the commission though." She had a distant look on her face.

"He just let it go to me. So I'd tuck a few dollars in his pocket just in case his Daddy wouldn't let him have the commission out of politeness but he'd say, 'no Miss Pam. That's yours for training me.'"

Hayden didn't know if she believed that Pam was responsible for Brian's knowledge, but she listened intently and after a moment Pam's smile fell away.

"One day, Brine's mama died of cancer. They didn't tell the kid just how sick his mama was until it was at the very end, so it was extra hard on him. He'd still come in here, but he was different. Just... not happy at all." Pam coughed and her mouth turned down in displeasure.

"Robert married one of the girls here two years later. And even though he didn't talk to me about it, I know Brine didn't like it." Pam stared at Hayden. "And that's what I remember."

Hayden was quiet as she absorbed the story with its abrupt ending. Finally, she shrugged. "He turned to drugs in his grief, but he also stole from his own father's company."

Pam nodded. "He was in charge of the print and distribution of the covers. Instead of sending out thirty-thousand, he would send out twenty-five-thousand and pocket the difference. And when his addiction cost more than his pay and the amount that he was syphoning from the company, he started distributing less and less covers. It went on for several years and then it got suspicious.

"His workers knew he was an addict, but when it all came out, Brian took the blame. He didn't try to pin it on anyone else. Robert was devastated. He had no idea and so he just tucked Brine away into rehab and handled the fallout himself. Brine got out of rehab and within a few months, he was using again.

"Robert's second wife was fit to be tied and wanted him to cut Brine off. So he did and Brine went away for a while. When he came back, he told his daddy that he was clean. There are some trust issues I'm sure. But Robert took him back and of course everyone expects him to fail, even Robert. But Brine has this... look on his face that he's never had before. It's like that look you had when you walked in the door that first day."

Hayden's brow furrowed as she gave Pam a confused look.

"It was a fierce look. Like... you already knew that this was just another hurdle. They call it determination, I guess. But that's how Brine looked when he came back this last time. Even though everybody is waiting for him to mess up, he hasn't. Whatever happened when he went away that last time straightened him out."

The two women sat quietly for a few more moments before Pam made to stand and return to work.

"Pam."

The older woman paused.

"Why did you set me up to fail?"

Pam stared at her. "Because I don't know or care about you."

That answer offended and angered Hayden. How dare this woman act like Hayden should be a better person, when she failed to apply that same standard to herself?

"You care about Fox Vinyl, don't you? Because you sure care a whole hell of a lot when Mr. Fox is around," Hayden snapped.

Pam didn't seem phased by her irritation. "I've been here for so many years and faces come and faces go. No one stays here more than three or four months, just a handful of us have been around since the beginning. But mostly people just come and go, year in and year out.

"In the beginning you teach them everything and they still do what they want, or they move on to something different. And finally, you just tell them enough for them to either decide to quit right then and there or... if they give a damn then they will make an effort to figure out the rest."

Pam got up and walked away. Hayden sat there a moment longer before she headed back to her own desk as well. Brian was writing a sale on the board. He wore a tired expression and Hayden pursed her lips and walked up to him.

"Are you going to collect the bonus this round?"

He gave her a surprised look before shaking his head. "No."

They both knew that he could win it. Yet she figured that if he did he just wouldn't accept the money.

She nodded and suddenly wanted to tell him that she was sorry for judging him and for her unfriendly behavior. However, those were not words that people said out loud; they just do things to make amends for their bad behavior instead. So Hayden looked away and then looked back at Brian, meeting his eyes. She wouldn't be like that, not in this throwaway year when everything she did was supposed to be the right thing to do.

"Brian, I heard about what happened to you and I behaved pretty badly because of it. I mean, I wasn't very friendly to you afterwards and I want to apologize to you for that."

He seemed surprised by her confession. "Hayden, it's okay. I truly don't expect much."

His cynical response saddened her. "Brian, I train myself to focus on positive thoughts so the fruits produced by my subconscious are ripe and rich instead of weeds that devour and swallow."

He stared at her as if she was insane.

Amused, she explained. "It's a self-affirmation. I say them daily. This is one I used to say at the beginning when I was struggling with... well, with my own problems."

The confused look cleared from his face. "Say it again?" he asked. She repeated it and Brian raised his brow and nodded. "Okay."

When she returned to her desk, she caught Pam's eyes and the other woman nodded in acknowledgment.

The Jazz Festival came and went. Briefly, Hayden thought about the fact that MyKell was there with someone else, listening to Frankie Beverly singing about "Joy and Pain," and holding someone else in his arms as they swayed to the music. Then the moment ended, and she moved on. A few days later, Brian got up and stood by her desk. When she looked up at him he spoke.

"I am more than my past, my mistakes, my faults, my circumstances, my struggles, or my diseases. I am a magnificent totality of imperfect parts only beautified by my choices, bravery and impact."

Marcus, who was do-wopping to some invisible song in his head, stopped cold in the middle of a do and a wop. He looked at

Brian and then Hayden and then seemed to recoil slightly before continuing on to his marijuana break.

Hayden ignored Marcus and just nodded enthusiastically at Brian. "That is a good one! I need that one too."

Brian agreed that it was one of the better affirmations that he had learned.

"So which one do you have for the day?" he asked her.

"Today's is: 'I feel. Deeply. Powerfully. Fully. I am gifted with the strength and power of my abundant feelings.'"

"Nice." He pulled out his cell phone. "I'll text it to you, and then you send me yours. What's your number?"

"Oh good idea!" She pulled out her cell phone and the two exchanged numbers and then affirmations.

A while later, her cell phone rumbled and she checked it.

"Question?"

It was Brian. She looked up and across the aisle at him, but he was talking on the phone and not paying attention to her. Okay…

She tapped out a response.

"Yes?"

"Why do you eat your dinner in your car every night?"

Her face felt warm. It wasn't an optimum situation, but she had no choice but to have dinner on the run. She generally finished her meal in the parking lot before coming inside. How would he know anyway? He was already inside by the time her shift started.

"What? You must be talking about someone else."

"Why don't you eat inside?"

"Okay, why are you texting me these questions?"

"Because I'm supposed to be working."

"Wait, are you on the phone with a customer?"

"Nope."

"Lol! Well who is on the other side of that phone?"

"My answering machine at home."

Hayden laughed out loud and when Abdullah looked at her curiously, she straightened her face and then dialed her home phone number.

"Okay... you're a bad influence. I'm doing it now too." Hayden pretended to be making a sales call as she discreetly texted into her phone, which was sitting on her lap beneath the desk.

"You're terrible at being sneaky Hayden. You actually have to sound as if someone is responding to you and not like you're just leaving an extremely long message on an answering machine. Now, back to my question. Eating, car, why?"

"Because I used to be the cleaning lady here, remember? I know how dirty this place is."

"You can eat at your desk, you know. You have the neatest desk in the entire building. Your desk is even neater than the empty desks!"

"Are you mocking me Brian Fox?"

"No... I have a motive."

Hayden peeked up at him but Brian was playing his role very well and was telling his customer that he would gladly hold while he got the person in charge of advertising.

"What is it?"

"I see the bag in your garbage from Boston Market sometimes. So when you go there, you could bring me a brisket dinner."

"Are you serious?"

"Yes. You might have noticed that I don't leave until its quitting time. I'm pretty tired of bag lunches. A hot meal would be nice every once in a while. I'd cook something and bring leftovers but...Well, Abdullah's lunch doesn't taste as good mixed with my own."

Hayden smiled. *"Yeah, that's not a problem. I can do that."*

The next day, Hayden brought Brian his brisket dinner and he insisted on paying for both his and hers. He wouldn't take no for an answer, and she finally accepted but stated if he tried doing that each time then she wouldn't bring him anything else. He grudgingly accepted her conditions and then carried his meal into the canteen. When he returned he appeared a lot happier.

Hayden began bringing him dinner each evening from whichever restaurant she visited on her way in. She would quickly scarf down her meal while driving or she'd finish up while parked. Brian seemed grateful for whatever he was brought and after he repaid her, he would carry it into the canteen.

After this went on for about two weeks, Hayden came in fifteen minutes earlier than usual. She was carrying two dinners this time – hers and his. From that point on, she had dinner with Brian each evening just as she had breaks and lunch with Dani during the day.

Hayden and Dani were preparing to stretch their legs at last break by taking a walk around the building. It was hot, but the humidity was tolerable. Hayden's cell phone rumbled and she retrieved it while Dani looked at her in curiosity.

"You got a new man, Hade?"

"What? No. This is my friend Brian."

"The heroin addict?"

Hayden regretted ever revealing Brian's story to Dani. She certainly hadn't told it with any intentions of Dani using that information to categorize him.

"Ex-heroin addict."

"Hmph... So what's he got to say?"

"Well, we share positive affirmations. He just sent me one." Hayden read it aloud. "'I am kindly welcoming, vulnerably open and spontaneously giving. I have a limitless capacity boundary-breaking heart for the collective sharing.'" Hayden was smiling until Dani stared at her in disbelief.

"Are you serious? He should just send you a text saying, 'Hey Hayden lets have wild monkey sex!'"

"What? Okay, you are sick. There is nothing sexual about that affirmation."

"It has a hidden meaning," Dani advised as they stepped into the elevator. "Read it again."

Hayden did.

"See? That part about limitless capacity, heart for collecting and sharing. *Sharing*. Girl that man wants to share himself with you!"

Hayden moved to her sent file and read another affirmation to her friend as they stepped out of the elevator into the lobby.

"'I am my own unique self; special, creative and wonderful.'" She tilted her brow up at her friend. "I sent that to him yesterday. Does that mean that I want to bump uglies with the man? No!"

Dani gave her a half smile. "Okay. Don't say I didn't warn you when you find a dozen roses on your desk one evening."

Hayden rolled her eyes.

When Hayden arrived at work that evening, she was carrying veggie chili from a local deli for herself and a double BLT and chips for Brian. She headed straight for the canteen where Brian had just finished cleaning one of the tables with disinfectant cleaner that Hayden had told him was in the cabinet. He'd bought her one of those expensive bottled waters that didn't seem any different than the stuff that came out of the tap for free. Yet since she didn't trust the water fountains here since the time she'd seen a man spitting his chewing tobacco into it, she didn't make too much of a fuss.

"What's up Hayden?"

"Hey Brian." She put their dinners on the table. "You leave any sales for me to make?"

"One or two." He sat down and opened his bag with its huge sandwich. "Mmmm. This looks good. Thanks, I'm starving."

"No problem."

She dipped her plastic spoon into her hot chili. It was delicious even if it was the middle of summer and their city was in the midst of a heat wave.

"Did you run today?" he asked and then took a bite of the sandwich.

"Yep. And I didn't stop once."

"How long?"

"40 minutes."

"Wow."

"Well it was just on the treadmill," she responded sheepishly.

"Hayden! Why do you do that?"

Her eyes widened at his sharp words. He put his sandwich down on the wrinkled wax paper and leaned forward. His grey eyes seemed to darken.

"Just take it."

Uh... "Take it?"

"The compliment I just gave you."

She looked at him, unsure of how to respond. Then she finally spoke honestly. "I don't like compliments."

Brian sat back in his chair and studied her. "What happened to you Hayden? Why the affirmations and the exercise *and* two jobs? Why do you have absolutely nothing more than that in your life? You know-"

Hayden abruptly stood up and walked out the room. She heard Brian's chair scrape back as he got up to follow her, but she quickened her steps and walked into the ladies room. With hands that trembled in anger she turned on the water to splash her warm face and the door opened. Brian came in, but he held up his hands to let her know that he meant no harm.

"Hayden, I'm sorry. I didn't mean to push, okay? It's just; I know that you know all about what happened to me and the trouble I got into. And I know that you're struggling with something, but you don't open up at all.

"I mean, we talk every single day about making each day better but you never..." He paused. "But I don't have any right to push. I'm sorry."

Hayden glanced at the water as it ran down the dark drain and then she turned it off. She looked at him, speaking calmly despite the thundering of her heart against her ribcage. She was mad at Brian and at herself for being mad about it.

"It's not a big deal. But it's *personal*. I've never asked you about getting high or your relationship with your dad because that's personal too."

He looked away and nodded and then backed out of the ladies room.

When Hayden returned to her desk, her chili, bottled water and purse were sitting on her desk. Brian was sitting at his desk typing on his computer. He didn't look at her.

~Chapter 9~
SWEET DREAMS

Brian got called into his father's office again and was still in there when Hayden left for the evening.

Why did this bother her so much? She didn't do anything wrong... did she? Hayden drove home in deep thought, feeling guilty and sad, but not sure why. Once home, she gathered the mail from her mailbox and stacked it neatly on the side table for sorting this weekend. She then prepared for her shower and afterwards climbed into bed.

Well, you did make Brian think that you were honest, but you're a liar, aren't you?

What? She considered that strange thought. She had lied? Then Hayden realized that she had discovered what was bothering her.

For months, she had strived to be honest with herself and by doing that she had reacted to people with honesty, particularly Brian when she apologized to him for judging him. Also when she shared aspirations and became a support system for him — one that he obviously was starving for. Damn...

I know you're struggling with something but you don't open up...

He had been waiting for her to trust in their friendship and to open up to him; instead she'd told him that he had no right to expect that. Hayden tossed in her bed until she sat up. Dammit! She reached for her cell phone.

"In April, my life was going as it always did. Until the morning that my boyfriend of six years told me that he had found someone else and was leaving me."

Hayden pressed send and the message was transported to Brian Fox's phone. However, she didn't wait for a response. She simply began texting more.

"I realized that I had been very clueless with no idea that the man I was with didn't want me anymore until the very second he told me. How long did he see me – this woman that he no longer loved, before he couldn't take it anymore?"

She looked at the phone and it's blank response screen. She took a deep breath. *Honesty...*

*"I began to see the **me** that I figured he must see. It was ugly. I was ugly and I had to find something more than that inside of me."*

She squeezed her eyes closed and pressed send. Then her cell phone suddenly rang shrilly, scaring her. She let it ring again before she answered, her eyes still closed in embarrassment.

"Me too," Brian said immediately. "When I thought about what I'd done to my dad, I saw someone ugly, someone that I didn't want to be, but I didn't know how to get away from that guy. The only way was to become something better... but not just for my dad, Hayden. For myself."

Hayden was nodding her head. "Yes! My friend thinks deep down that it's to get revenge on my ex, or so that I can find someone else. That is so far from the truth. All I want is to not be disgusted by the person that I am."

"You're doing what it takes to make that happen. We both are. There's no messing up. I lose everything if I mess up."

Hayden understood that so deeply. "If I mess up, then I'm not capable of being anything better. And I'm not going to be a walking mistake waiting to happen."

"Me neither," Brian responded quietly.

After a moment of quiet, Hayden spoke again. "It's hard."

"Yes, it is. And that's why we will value it all the more when we finally make it."

She stared ahead as if seeing her friend, the person that shared so much of her same pain. It was as if the words he spoke were her own. She almost hadn't opened up to him, and if that had happened, then she wouldn't be feeling this relief in her soul now.

They talked for a while before Brian told her to go to sleep.
"Yeah, I better."
"Sweet dreams Hayden."
She smiled. "You too Brian."

They were gearing up for a new monthly bonus contest. Brian hadn't won the last one; it had been a man from a different team. Instead of a thousand bucks, this month's prize was a gas card good for one fill-up a week for the next year.

That was something that would come in handy, even though her commissions had been rolling in and Hayden was quickly paying off credit card after credit card with them. She got out of her car carrying two turkey specials from The Cracker Barrel. She noticed Marcus quickly climb out of his car when he saw her hands were filled. She was grateful because she had become paranoid about being the only person coming in at this shift even though it was still light out at 6:00 P.M. Yet she had noticed that each and every night there was a strange car parked there with a man sitting in it doing nothing.

That wouldn't normally be strange, after all, it was a strip mall parking lot. However, she'd been working in this building for months before being employed by Fox Vinyl, so she was used to getting here at 6:00 P.M. to start cleaning the top floor offices. Then each and every night, she had been forced to return to her car to wait impatiently for Fox Vinyl to empty. So Hayden knew for a fact that there hadn't ever been any other cars parked with men sitting in them at that time. This was a recent development.

She suspected drug sales were discreetly being done here and by people other than Marcus. Covington was a hotbed of drug activity. Marcus hurried ahead of her to open the door to the building. He didn't smell like weed at the moment, so she figured he stayed with pills until it was dark enough to hide his smoking activities.

"Mmmm. That smells good," he said while staring her coolly in the eye. "What makes some men lucky enough to get the special treatment? And more importantly, how do I get that service?"

She bristled at the cold look on his face. She also didn't care for his words and innuendo. "My *friends* know the answer to those questions," she responded, giving him the same cool look.

His mouth turned up into a quick smile. "I'm just playing with you." Then he laughed before he pimp walked back to his desk, being very obnoxious about it.

Buffoon… Hayden headed to the canteen and when Brian saw her, he began rubbing his hands together in anticipation for his turkey dinner. She couldn't stop the giggle that fell from her lips.

Over the weeks he had filled out considerably and looked healthy the way he must have been pre-addiction. He had apparently caught some rays because his once pale skin glowed with a golden tan and his blondish brown hair was now blonder than brown. He still wore long sleeved shirts; mostly polo style and she wished that he wasn't ashamed to show his arms with their evidence of his past addiction. However, that was something he had to do in his own time.

"I got you the green beans and mashed potatoes with brown gravy."

"Green beans?"

"Well yeah. What? You want the turnip greens instead?"

"I hate vegetables; except for mashed potatoes or coleslaw. Or corn on the cob. Oh and relish."

She sat down and shook her head. "But that's turkey and dressing. You can't go without a veggie!"

He shook his head. "It's not Thanksgiving. You only have to eat veggies with turkey and dressing on Thanksgiving Day."

Hayden began to mix her gravy and dressing together. "Brian, the only reason that you don't like veggies is because you've never eaten any that I've cooked. You probably eat that canned stuff."

She took a bite of food savoring the flavor of each side dish piled on her fork. "I make this smothered cabbage with onions and bacon. It's *so* good." She reached for a corn muffin—only one allowed. "With meatloaf, it's heavenly."

Brian wasn't eating right now; he was just watching her as she talked with food pooching out one cheek, expertly keeping everything inside of her moving mouth. "Yes. I'm game, I guess. When?"

"When?" She squinted.

"When are you going to show me how to make it? Sunday is a good day for me. Then you can come over and I'll do all the cooking if you do all the teaching. Just write out a list of ingredients and I'll pick them up when I go grocery shopping."

She crooked her head at him, but he was serious. "You want me to come to your house and cook?"

"No silly woman. I want you to come to my house and show me how to cook it. I want you to sit down and rest or something."

Then he turned his attention back to his food, obviously ignoring the green beans. Hayden looked at him periodically, suspiciously.

The next day while at her first job, Hayden's cell phone vibrated announcing a new text message had been delivered. She discreetly checked her cell phone while talking to a customer. Cell phone use during work was a strict no-no.

It was from Brian. She began reading it while her customer continued to explain in detail something that she didn't care about and didn't need to know. She let the woman ramble on while she read.

"Family may misunderstand me, but kindred spirits abound and I trust that my soul sought the home it needed for growth, expansion, lessons unlearned, mysteries unsolved, and elevations yet unknown."

Hayden gasped.

"Excuse me?" Her customer paused.

"Oh, I mean I believe I have enough information. Ma'am, may I place you on hold to research?"

"Research? What are you going to research?"

"Just a minute... uh... we have some new procedures." Hayden quickly pressed hold on her phone and then re-read the message. *What the-?* Hayden looked frantically over at Dani, but she was busy talking to her own customer. Oh crap, did this affirmation mean what she thought it did?

"Wow," she texted back. *"That's a very good one."* She waited a few moments, but he didn't text anything else. *Oh crap, my customer!*

"Sorry about the hold ma'am..." Oh what in the hell had they been talking about?

By the time Hayden arrived at her second job, she was very frazzled and knew that she was acting as awkward as she felt. "So, I got us Italian wedding soup... with the meatballs," she said. Then she hurried into the canteen where Brian was waiting with her expensive water and his can of soda.

"Mmmm, good."

She bumped her cup of soup and if Brian hadn't grabbed it, she would've lost the entire thing instead of the small amount that splashed onto the table. "Oh damn!" She jumped up to get paper napkins.

"Hold on, I still got napkins over here from cleaning the table." Brian wiped up the mess. "Sit down, I got it."

She took her seat again and reached for her bottled water and tipped it over instead. Luckily she hadn't opened it yet. "Oh damn!"

Brian gave her a curious look. "Hayden calm down, I got it. Did you have a bad day?"

"Oh..." Hayden's eyes met his and locked. For some reason she couldn't look away.

"Are you okay?"

She nodded quickly.

Brian began eating his soup, and a moment later she did the same.

"So what's your affirmation today?"

"Oh..." she said again and he looked at her.

"You didn't text yours back to me."

"Mine is..." she struggled to bring the words to mind. "Be filled with wonder. Be touched by peace."

He stared at her. His eyes were so...

"Beautiful," Brian said.

Her eyes flitted away before she allowed her gaze to meet his again, and it was like a gentle caress that did something to her stomach and made her breathing difficult. He smiled slowly and then returned to eating his soup. Hayden ate the rest of her soup, but she didn't feel like smiling. Not one bit.

That night as Hayden lay in bed; she tossed and turned trying not to think of the affirmation that kept rolling through her mind. She punched her pillow and then spoke the words mentally, angrily, already knowing what she had to do.

My need to be comfortable isn't as important as living in my truth.

She picked up her cell phone and began to text Brian.

~Chapter 10~
LIVING IN THE TRUTH

Todd gave Hayden a curious look as they ran on the treadmills side-by-side. Finally he stopped his and climbed down. Then he pressed the controls to slow Hayden's. She looked at him in surprise for a moment before it came to a complete stop.

"Are you okay?" he asked.

"What?"

"You've been running hard for nearly the entire time. What happened to intervals?"

"I was?" She couldn't believe that, but she had been so deep in thought that she had forgotten to switch down to a fast walk. She didn't even realize that she could run like that without even feeling it. For a moment, she put aside the thoughts that had been nagging her this morning. Besides, the conversation that she'd had with Brian last night was bad enough without continuing to rehash it.

"Fifty K here I come!" she said with forced enthusiasm.

"Yes, you're doing better than good. Bad news though, this weekend I won't be able to meet you at the park. My shift at the fire station takes up both days this weekend."

"Oh, that's fine." She tried not to sound disappointed. She had grown to enjoy her time in the park with Kevin and Todd. The little boy was hungry to prove himself to his stepfather.

Hayden especially enjoyed watching Todd freak out when Kevin got on the rocks over the creek or when he jumped a pole and missed, falling face first and busting his lip. Todd looked like he would pass out. He would have carried the boy back to the truck, but a short time later, Kevin was up and running around again.

Todd had just looked at her in anguish. "I don't think I'm going to survive being a father."

Yeah, she would miss them this weekend.

"Well, you have to work, but that doesn't mean the partnership has to stop. I can pick up Kevin and we'll train without you."

Todd smiled at her and shook his head. "We live too far away. We can make it up, though."

"Alright. Well I'll still be there same time same place."

He nodded. "I know you will. You're doing good Hayden."

She started to roll her eyes, but then stopped herself. "Thanks Todd."

As Hayden parked in the lot of Fox Vinyl, she wished she could just turn her car around and go back home so that she wouldn't have to face Brian tonight. Last night's conversation had been bad, but even worse than the conversation had been the implications that had gone unspoken. Last night she had done the stupidest thing imaginable and she wished with all her heart that she could take it back.

Hayden had picked up her cell phone last night. She sent a quick text to Brian.

"I can't sleep."

Almost immediately, she received a response even though it was well after 1:00 A.M.

"Why?"

"Because I have something on my mind and… I can't stop thinking about it."

"Can I help?"

"I think so. It's a question I have for you."

"Oh?"

"Yeah. I need to know something. Brian, are you attracted to me?"

There was a long pause. It was so long that she wondered if he had turned off his phone or something.

Five long minutes after asking the question a text came through.

"Hayden. I'm not."

Her face burned as she read the words.

"I mean, we're friends and of course I care about you, but it's not like that. For me, attraction is what develops after I know someone as a friend."

Hayden put down her phone and climbed out of bed, pacing back and forth as she covered her mouth. *Oh my god… what have I done?*

Brian must think she was a nutcase. After all, they were friends who knew the worst about each other. They could pal around, eat dinner together and then one day she looked into his eyes and felt something that went deeper than friendship; all because she had confused his attention for something more.

There were tears of regret in her eyes and she wiped them and returned to the phone where she began to read the rest of his texts. He sent a few of them in succession that she didn't answer:

"I'm not saying that it wouldn't happen at some point in the future. But…"

"Are you there?"

"I'm really sorry Hayden. This is really a shitty time in my life and maybe we should both focus on just moving to a better place within ourselves."

"Hayden?"

"Look, I'll see you tomorrow."

That last message had been sent a minute ago. She quickly responded.

"I just didn't want there to be any confusion, that's all. We're just friends. Nothing more."

"Okay. You had me worried there for a minute," came his response.

She closed her eyes, feeling the sting of rejection... again...

"Talk to you tomorrow."

When Hayden walked into the canteen she hoped that she wouldn't look at Brian and feel that strange sensation that she'd felt the day before. He met her eyes and there seemed to be caution etched there. Her heart sped up at the sight of him, and it was the most unwelcomed feeling possible.

"Hi," he greeted her.

"Hey, how's it going?" This was pretending. This wasn't real. It was just a means to get through this terrible year.

They ate their dinner more subdued than normal. Eventually, Brian cleared his throat. "Do you want to hear today's affirmation?"

She looked up, but avoided staring directly into those gray eyes that seemed to be able to see right down into her very soul. "Sure."

"It seems like I found this one when I really needed it." He began to recite it to her. "'In order to succeed I must imagine myself as already healthy, or as someone who has already overcome a challenge.'"

She let that sink in. "That is more than a daily affirmation. Sometimes you find ones that hit home and then it becomes like... your mission's motto instead of just a daily one. I have one that applies to my entire purpose too."

His brow rose in interest.

She looked down at her hands as she repeated it, pretending to struggle with her memory, but she had never, and would never, forget this affirmation. "'I am perfectly imperfect. I strive for better while loving all that I am today. In loving myself today, I am better equipped to improve myself tomorrow.'"

Brian was quiet. "That seems perfect for you." He cleared his throat again. "I'm going to hit the restroom. I'll talk to you later."

He carried his trash to the already overflowing can and smashed it down into it. She watched him despite not wanting to feel the attraction that had not abated, but had instead just grown stronger.

Just because someone says something nice to me, doesn't mean that they're falling in love with me...

She got up leaving her partially eaten meal on the table for someone else to clean up.

She had made two sales already tonight and almost mechanically she began the search for the next call. The sale didn't give her joy; it was just about getting to the money. Her eyes were scanning the phonebook page under pet stores when the front door of the building was pushed open hard enough to cause it to groan and the glass to rattle. She looked up in time to see blue suited bodies swarming inside.

Her team was closest to the entrance, so it was Pam's scream at the sight of the guns drawn that brought the beginning of chaos.

"SWAT! Stand with your hands visible! *Now!*"

A gun was pointed at her and she quickly came to her feet and held her hands up. It seemed like an endless flow of SWAT members swarmed into the office. She looked at Brian. His face was totally white, but he was standing with his hands behind his head. An officer was patting him down!

Oh my God... Brian?

Another officer was patting down Abdullah while someone else had Marcus face down on his desk and was putting handcuffs on him! As Hayden looked around, she saw that every man was being searched and the women were asked to open their purses.

"Ma'am, I need to see inside your purse!"

A tall man was pointing his gun just over her head, but she knew that he would aim it at her and have her shot in the split second where she could do anything foolish. Hayden nodded quickly and still showing one hand she opened her drawer and retrieved her purse slowly. Another man dumped the contents on her desk, and then searched every single crevice and opened every single container; including her hand lotion which was dumped on the floor.

Mr. Fox was standing by his office with a scared, shocked look on his face. He too had gone white and two uniformed officers were talking to him in low tones. Someone began shouting, and then there were suddenly several officers on the floor along with a big man who seemed to be having a seizure. Wires were protruding from his body connected to something held in another officer's hand.

He had been tazed. He was red faced and struggling while the cuffs were placed on him and he was brought up to a standing position. Hayden was shaking as they began to escort the handcuffed individuals from the building. Nine employees of Fox Vinyl and Map Ads were piled into a waiting van, and included in that count were two women.

She was looking at Brian who seemed shocked that he wasn't included in the people escorted out. He just kept looking around in disbelief and then Mr. Fox hurried to him and grabbed him in a hug.

"It wasn't you, son. It wasn't about you..." came the older man's muffled sobs.

Brian comforted his father, rubbing his shoulders and saying, "It's okay now Dad. It's over, okay? We're okay..."

The men in the parking lot! Those were cops that had been watching Fox Vinyl! If she'd seen them then Brian and Mr. Fox had probably spotted them as well. However, where she had concluded that the men were drug dealers, the two of them knew it for what it really was; surveillance. Only they must have thought it was to take down Brian even though the case was closed. Yet, hadn't she heard somewhere that Federal cases never really closed?

Pam's soft sobs caught her attention. The older woman was stooped on the floor picking up her personal items from where they had been dumped by the police. Hayden moved around her desk and helped Pam pick up her things even though Hayden's own items were still scattered all over her desk and the floor too.

"Are you okay, Pam? They didn't hurt you, did they?"

She shook her head and sniffed back her tears. "Just pissed me off. Having a gun pointed at me..."

Hayden nodded in agreement.

"Listen everyone," Mr. Fox had his hands up trying to get his employees' attention. "I want everybody to go home. We'll be open for business tomorrow. I just want you to know that I'm sorry for... this mess!" He sounded disgusted.

Hayden gathered her things quickly. She wanted nothing more than to get home or just away from all of this...

"Hayden!"

Brian hurried across the aisle to her. He just grabbed her shoulders, a smile on his face.

"It wasn't about me!" He pulled her into his arms. His heart was beating hard and his arms around her body almost made her weak. "I thought it was about me..." he mumbled.

After a moment she slid from his grasp, untangling herself from his hold. She smiled slightly at him, nodding her head. "No, it wasn't you, Brian."

Mr. Fox was suddenly there and he put his hand on his son's shoulder. The relief in his face confirmed her thoughts about what the two of them had been thinking.

"I better go," she said as she turned to leave.

"But Hayden, I thought-"

"We'll talk tomorrow." She glanced at Mr. Fox and then she walked out the door.

~Chapter 11~
HELLA MONEY

"What's your friend's name? The one that you've been trying to get me to meet?"

Dani's eyes moved to Hayden's and then she lowered the donut that was headed for her open mouth.

"Sean!"

"Is he still single?"

"Yes! Do you want to meet him?"

Hayden nodded and when Dani did the happy dance in her seat, Hayden couldn't help the laughter that bubbled up and out of her. Dani was a good friend who cared about her. Why hadn't she allowed the possibility that Dani might just have been able to help her get through the heartache after her breakup with MyKell?

Hayden continued to nod her head. "Yes, I would like to meet Sean. Tell me some more about him."

Dani sang his praise. Tall, dark, extremely handsome, had a good job, his own home and on and on and on...

"Come over this weekend. We'll have a barbecue Saturday and I'll introduce you two."

"Okay, I will."

"Uh... Hayden."

"What?"

"It's time to go shopping for some more clothes."

Hayden looked down at herself. She had lost a lot more weight... Well, wasn't that the reason she worked out six days a week? However, her routine was now so ingrained into her that she no longer thought about the reason, only making sure it got done.

She exhausted herself by working a second job, which had paid off all but her largest credit card. Her home was spotless; she never had time to mess it up. Her mind was finally at peace and she didn't have to fight with herself any longer when she read her daily affirmations.

"Yeah," she said in surprise. It was September. She counted the months since that day in April when she had looked at her calendar and had made the decision to throw away an entire year of her life. Five months down already...

When Hayden arrived at her second job carrying meatloaf sandwiches, she was surprised to see that the office was nearly empty. Even with the nine people that had been carted away yesterday, there should have still been more employees present. However, right now, she counted only seven people – including Brian, Pam, Abdullah and herself.

She didn't bother going to the canteen because she could see Brian was busy on a call. He wasn't sitting at his desk either, but was on the other side of the room. What was up with that? Not that she needed to constantly look up just to see him watching her... or vice versa.

She went over to where he was sitting and placed his dinner on his desk. He looked at her and raised his hand in silent apology. His eyes darted around the room and she got the message; *too busy to stop for dinner.*

Before she could even sit down, Mr. Fox came over to her. "May I talk to you, Hayden?"

"Oh. Sure, sir." Uh oh. Did she mess something up?

When she was in his office he had her sit in the plastic chair while he sat down behind his desk. He looked very tired and not very happy.

"Hayden, I just want to thank you for coming in today. We had several people call off and some even quit." He drummed his fingers along his desk in a way that Brian did when he was tense.

"I heard from the police this morning. Yesterday was about a drug sting. Marcus Miller and several others have been arrested for either possessing controlled substances or for the distribution of them. After the arrests, we're very short-staffed. I don't know how we're going to close the current campaigns, let alone get to the upcoming ones." He was quiet for a moment and Hayden felt for him, but at least he wasn't mad at her about anything, so she relaxed a little.

"I was wondering if there is anyway that you can work extra hours? I know you have a full time job, but I need my experienced sales team to push out the orders. I'm willing to pay you a salary plus commission if you would consider increasing your hours."

He considered her one of his experienced sellers? She felt a sense of pride and accomplishment at his words, but regardless, how was she going to put in more hours when she already worked 12 hours a day? Even worse was how could she turn down the money he was talking about?

"I'm going to open the office on the weekends. If you would do eight more hours it would be helpful. If not... I do understand."

She could manage giving up some hours on her weekends. "What time would you want me here?"

His eyes looked hopeful. "Whatever shift you want, or you wouldn't have to follow a shift. Just come in and work your eight hours, split any way you want, but email me when you come in and let me know when you leave, so that I can keep track of your hours. And if you do that Hayden, I'll pay you a salary for all of your hours and you would still collect your full commissions." Thirty percent commissions plus being salaried was astounding!

Hayden nodded. "I can do that."

He looked relieved. "I'll get you your own key before the end of the week." He discussed his plans to hire more people and asked her if she would help train a new team. Evidently Abdullah and Pam would also be training new teams as well.

"I would be honored to do that Mr. Fox."

He apologized and then told her that she would be working the remainder of a different phonebook. When she returned to her seat, she realized that not one of the people from the team whose phonebook she was working on now was present. She looked over their board and then in disbelief realized the number of re-runs yet to be called. Hayden smiled in genuine pleasure. Oh she was about to make hella money!

Usually, if Hayden was working a city where she had to stop making calls because it was after business hours, she was supposed to finish up all her paperwork instead. However, Mr. Fox said that all the Telemarketing people were to do was to make calls and that the credit card and printing departments would take over anything dealing with paper. So Hayden switched to sales in Shoreline, Washington at 9:00 P.M. and continued selling re-runs until she finally stopped at 10:30 P.M. She ended her day with seven sales! That was over a grand in commissions in just one day!

When she left that evening, she was exhausted, but hyped. Still, she couldn't wait to fulfill her date with her pillow. Just then, Brian came running out of the building after her.

"Hayden!"

She stopped and waited for him to catch up.

"Hey." He combed his fingers through his unruly hair.

"Hey."

"I wanted to talk to you. My dad and I have been here almost around the clock trying to get things in order and I've barely had a break. Do you have a minute?"

She inhaled, wishing she could lie and say no. "Okay, but I have to get home-"

"I won't be long, I promise."

He chewed his lip as he stared at her. "When you texted me that question..."

She looked away feeling her stomach sink. It was almost like the day MyKell had told her that he had met someone else. She did not want to do this again.

"Brian-"

"It was after my dad had called me into his office to tell me about a van that had been parked on his street off and on for the past few weeks. It was a white cargo van and it really stood out. I told him about seeing people sitting in their cars across the street and sometimes in the lot. That's when we knew that we were being watched by the police."

She nodded. "I noticed the people in the cars, too. But I thought they were drug dealers."

"Hayden I thought I was about to be sent to federal prison. Jail time for mail fraud can be up to twenty years for each count." He gnawed his lip in despair.

"I went home that night and thought about using. I even had the phone in my hand thinking about calling my old dealer. And then I got your text. My heart kind of leapt and suddenly I was just focused on what was wrong with you. Drugs have never given me the peace that talking to you does and I realized that no matter what, that was always going to be the truth."

Hayden was shocked. She searched his eyes.

"Then you asked me that question; was I attracted to you. I started texting how I think about you constantly. How beautiful you are and how you don't even seem to know."

Hayden's mouth fell open; butterflies began to form in her belly at Brian's words and the intensity of his stare. Then he placed his gentle hands on her shoulders. "I wrote that I'm more than attracted to you Hayden, and that every day you keep me grounded. That you motivate me and that all I want to do is to inspire you in return. I don't want you to throw away a year of your life—not one second of your life, because who you are now is the person that I'm falling in love with."

Hayden couldn't breathe. She was frozen, staring at him in disbelief, nearly trembling. Falling in love... He said that he was falling in love... with her.

His face darkened. "But what I couldn't do was figure out how to tell you that I was about to face prison time; and a long sentence too. And that's when I knew that I couldn't do that. I couldn't do that to you. I wouldn't want you throwing away ten or twenty years of your precious life on someone that wouldn't be here."

He looked away, his hands still holding her. "I don't ever want you to miss me when I'm gone. I don't want you to worry about me when I'm gone. And I don't want you haunted by what could have been..."

He met her eyes again. "I wrote what I did, hoping we could... I don't know. I was wishing that I hadn't allowed myself to feel the way I did for you and wishing that it could go back to when we were just friends. I didn't want to hurt you. I just didn't know how to make it go back to the way it was before..."

Hayden shook her head. She needed to get her thoughts straight, to absorb all that she was feeling, to know if there was something that she wasn't seeing. Brian held onto her hand not allowing her to retreat and when she looked down at his hand wrapped around hers she felt her emotions unraveling.

"I'm sorry Hayden. Don't leave-"

She felt a shuddering sob and when Brian refused to let her go she covered her face with her free hand.

"I thought I'd messed up," she cried. "I thought I had misread the signs. I thought I would never learn how to read the signs that were right in front of my face."

Brian gently placed his hand on her chin until she looked up at him. He was shaking his head. "What I noticed about you is that you don't read the same signs that the rest of us see. You are uniquely you."

Hayden stared at him, making sure that she was seeing what was truly before her eyes.

Brian's mouth tilted up into a soft smile. "And yes, it did take you a long time to see the signs. I sent you affirmations of love. I sent you messages about how wonderful you were. I freaking... hijacked your Sunday and you still didn't get it!"

She laughed and reached up to wipe the tears that spilled down her cheeks, but Brian bent down and kissed one damp cheek and then the other until he had kissed them all away. The sudden onslaught of desire almost caused her knees to weaken. Brian's lips inched towards hers, where he lightly kissed them. Her toes curled in her shoes when she heard his soft sigh of pleasure. His touch was very gentle; like a feather's touch. Before long, his kiss deepened and became sensual when his tongue brushed hers and soon he was sucking her lips—first the top and then the bottom.

He pulled back suddenly, putting his hands on her shoulders, almost as if to hold her at bay.

"Sorry, I'm..."

She smiled. "Sorry?"

He shook his head adamantly. "No. Not sorry, but..." He suddenly smiled. "You know, you never answered me."

Hayden thought back but didn't remember being asked anything. She gave him a questioning look.

"You never said whether or not you'll come over Sunday for meatloaf and smothered cabbage."

She clenched down low. This was one of those hints that she hadn't caught earlier. She returned his mischievous smile. "Well, I'll come over if you really cook me some meatloaf and cabbage."

He watched her lips as he gnawed on his own. She could see that it was taking all of his control not to kiss her again. She wished that his control was just a little weaker.

He inhaled deeply. "I'll text you my address." He finally allowed his hands to drop from her shoulders, and Hayden stood nearly swaying as their connection ended.

"See you tomorrow Hayden."

She nodded, staring deeply into his eyes that she couldn't seem to get enough of. "Goodnight Brian." Then before he could leave, she gave in to her desire and placed her hands around his waist, leaned in and kissed him gently.

Brian's hands immediately moved to the back of her head. His fist was suddenly buried in the thick mass of coils. "Oh damn, Hayden..." he muttered, "I think about you constantly." His mouth claimed hers as his kisses became frenzied. Hayden grimaced nearly in pain at his words—and not just the words but also the honesty in them. He desired her, he wanted her, and he was falling in love with her.

Trembling, this time it was her that pulled back. He allowed his hands to drop but he continued to lightly gnaw his lip as if he missed the contact there. She didn't say anything else as she turned gracelessly and headed for her car, hoping that she wouldn't stumble because her legs didn't seem able to work right now.

~Chapter 12~
NO PROMISES, NO LIES

It was the best week of Hayden's life, despite the fact that she did things that most would consider tedious; however, she was now doing it with much more ease. She worked out each morning, pounding the treadmill in a steady jog—no intervals, just full out running. Then it was on to her first job, where she spent most of the day looking forward to going in to her second job.

She was making money hand-over-fist there and the new crew that she trained were fast learners. Unfortunately, one woman had already quit after learning about the new drug-testing policy and another had sold a re-run belonging to another employee. Hayden was just happy that it wasn't Abdullah's re-run because that would have just been too ironic.

After thinking about it long and hard, Hayden made the woman return the commission, even though the guy it rightfully belonged to sheepishly told her to keep it. Then after that, it was pretty clear that Hayden had made a new enemy of the woman— at least until the woman discovered that the boss' son had the hots for Hayden... The money was great of course, but the real highlight of her day was seeing Brian. However, there was little time to do much more than exchange brief greetings. With their backlog of work, neither took the time to eat dinner in the canteen and just ate separately at their desks between calls.

He stopped at her desk whenever possible, but it was obvious that he wanted to be kissing her and not just talking. He continuously asked her if she was still coming for dinner Sunday, and she had to assure him that she was looking forward to it. She didn't mention the fact that Saturday she was going to be meeting another man.

It was a terribly screwed up situation, but one that she couldn't change now without damaging her friendship with Dani. Hayden didn't realize just how much her new lifestyle had affected her friendship. She explained all that had happened from the drug bust to Brian's admission of love, her face showing how thrilled she was about the new romantic path that she was taking. Hayden was ready to speculate about interracial dating and how wonderful kissing Brian had been. She was also ready to explore why he felt the way he did for her and why she felt the way she did for him. Unfortunately, the conversation had just gone sideways.

"Oh my God... this is unreal." Dani looked floored.

"Dani... I think I'm falling in love with Brian." Hayden's face filled with an impossibly large smile.

"Hayden! What about my friend Sean? I mean, I already invited him to a barbecue Saturday and I've been talking you up like crazy. He was really looking forward to meeting you!"

Hayden was surprised into silence. How could Dani honestly be talking about this guy Sean when she was telling her that she was falling in love? Alright, so maybe it wasn't love—maybe it was something different, but she wanted to at least talk about that possibility with her friend. What did Sean have to do with anything when Hayden had found someone that she connected with?

Hayden raised her hands. "I'm sorry Dani. I don't need to meet Sean when I'm already interested in Brian. Besides that, I told you that I'm working Saturday-"

"Fine." Dani threw up her hands. "Forget it, just forget it," Dani said before she angrily gathered up the remains of her uneaten lunch.

"Dani-?"

Her friend shook her head. "Hayden, am I just some interference in your life? Because you treat me like you *have* to deal with me. I'm not even talking about the fact that we barely hang out anymore, that you don't call me, and that I can't call you, but even when we're taking breaks together, you're not even here."

Hayden's mouth parted. How could Dani be saying this when she knew what Hayden's schedule was like? Anger at her friend's selfishness began to build within her.

"Hayden, I miss you," Dani's eyes sparkled. "Where are you? You're not here. You think I can't see that you've pulled back from me? I do want you to meet Sean, but the biggest thing is that I just want you to come to the barbecue because I miss having fun with you."

The anger that had been building suddenly receded at the sight of Dani's honesty. Yes, Hayden had retreated and she hadn't trusted their friendship enough to talk to her best friend about how she was feeling. Hayden sighed.

"It's not you Dani. It's me. I didn't know that I was doing that to you." Hayden looked into the air. It was hard to say the words that she was thinking, but she had to anyway. "In a way, I'm trying to save my life. I'm trying to find something in me that I can learn to love and respect, and day by day, I'm finally finding it."

Dani touched her hand. "Hayden, you are a good person. You think that just because you look a certain way that it defines who you are, but you are better than that. Why would you let a man make you doubt who you are? MyKell was a user and this guy Brian, he might not be the same kind of user, but he's got a questionable history-"

"Wait-"

"*And* a questionable future. You even said that he expected the Feds to still come after him. Plus he's a heroin addict-"

"Ex-"

"Sweetheart, there is no such thing as an 'ex' when it comes to heroin addiction. You are always an addict that is just one needle prick away from falling back into it. You do realize that the need *never* goes away. It's something that he will always have to fight."

Hayden became irritated again that Dani wasn't willing to listen… and then she realized that both of them were guilty of not listening. Didn't she recently chide herself for shutting out her friends? She and Dani were her friends for a reason. So Hayden shut her mouth and she listened quietly and actively, despite how badly she wanted to jump up and defend Brian and her feelings for him.

"Hayden, we always go back to what we know. Now I know MyKell wasn't a druggy, but he was a *user*. All I'm saying is that Sean has a lot going for him and at the very least; you could just stop by after you leave work. You wouldn't have to stay long. Just meet him with an open mind, and if you still feel as if you aren't interested, then no harm, no foul. So if there's no attraction, then oh well."

Hayden took a moment to digest her friend's words and then she stared into Dani's eyes. "Okay, I'll come to the barbecue after work."

Dani smiled.

"Because you're right, we don't hang out the way we used to and I miss that too. I'll even meet Sean because he's a friend of yours and you want me to meet him. But some of what you said to me was wrong Dani. When you tell me what I am, what I should see when I look in the mirror, and what I should feel, it means that I was right in not discussing my feelings with you."

Dani gave her a surprised look.

"It means that you have no concept of how deeply I have grown to hate the person that I see in the mirror, and how much I hate being in my own skin. If that's all it would take to fix what's broken in me, then I wouldn't spend every waking moment of my life fighting to be something else. So I don't need *you* to tell me who *I* am. I need to be the one to tell *myself* this. With those affirmations that you think are so stupid, I have been learning to feel good about me again.

"And I was able to share those affirmations with a person who is learning to feel good about himself too. Whether we win, or whether we lose, we're both more than our past mistakes. So as much as I appreciate how much you care about me, it's not as much as I'm learning to care about myself."

Dani was quiet for a while. "You've come a long way Hayden. I'm sorry and I'll stop trying to make you into what I want to be."

After a moment Hayden nodded and then she gave her friend a stern look. "*And* you will need to stop with the criticizing of a man that you've never even met. Now it doesn't hurt me to go to the barbecue and meet Sean—but mostly because there's a big steak involved. But I warn you that I'm pretty sure about my feelings for Brian." Then a smile cancelled out Hayden's scowl. "He's the man I think I want to be with."

Dani smiled too. "To be in love. I remember that feeling."

"You get rid of Dante and you might discover it again." Dani gave her a surprised look, but Hayden just raised her hand innocently. "I'm just saying."

"Wow... I'm such a hypocrite, aren't I?"

"We don't generally see our mistakes as well as we see others'. Just keep being proud of you because that has been my goal since the beginning; to be proud of me."

When the alarm clock went off Saturday morning, Hayden seriously thought about not going to the gym. However, she knew that the first time she made an excuse would just be the first step in causing all of her discipline to unravel. So she staggered out of bed, made an egg white omelet for breakfast, and then went into auto-pilot through her workout and preparations for her four hour shift.

It felt strange to drive into Fox Vinyl's parking lot at 8:00 A.M. and on a Saturday. She figured that she could work until noon and then go shopping for something to wear that actually fit. Then she would hit the barbecue, meet Dani's friend, and leave shortly after.

She walked to the office holding her new key, but the door was already unlocked and Brian, Abdullah and a few others were already present. When Brian looked up and saw her, he grinned and came over to greet her.

"You're a sight for sore eyes." He looked tired, but even near exhaustion he couldn't hide the look of pleasure on his face.

"Oh? And why is that?"

"Because no one from the credit card company showed up today. I have to go there and take over and I don't want to leave this place in the hands of," he leaned in to whisper, "Abdullah."

"What? You want me to be in charge? Where's your Dad?"

"He'll be here at noon. Hayden, he really needed the rest. He's only been going home long enough to clean up and then he's been sleeping in his office. But don't worry, he trusts you. All you'd have to do is make sure that no one goofs around and that everything is running smoothly."

She nodded in disappointment. "Of course I'll do it... but I thought I was going to get to look at you all day." She loved gazing at Brian, especially when she looked up and saw that he was already watching her. It made the day special and caused her to feel just like a teenager with a first crush.

Brian looked around quickly and then gave her a quick peck on the cheek. "I know honey. Me too. But I'll get to see you tomorrow — and more importantly, I get a home cooked meal."

"No. *I* get a home cooked meal. You get to cook it. Did you go to the grocery store yet?"

"Not yet, I'll be doing that after work tonight. Look, I better get going. Text you later?"

"You better." She smiled.

Four hours moved quickly with everyone taking advantage of the opportunity to make rapid calls and rapid sales. If not for the barbecue, Hayden would've stayed longer, but as soon as Mr. Fox arrived, she sent him a quick hello, which was also a goodbye email, and left. Then Hayden quickly headed for a department store that she had always found too expensive for her budget. However, this time she browsed for several outfits that she liked without even checking the price tags. As an afterthought, she also selected sexy underwear; things that she had always liked from afar but would not have been able to squeeze her body into.

She thought about Brian too, imagining him looking at her in them and her face grew flushed. Tomorrow she could kiss him again. Would she... have sex with him if things headed in that direction? She wanted to think ahead because she already knew that things would most definitely head in that direction if she had anything to do with it.

When Hayden arrived at Dani and Dante's apartment later in the evening, she was dressed in a long, slimming, spaghetti strap sundress. She had taken a length of colorful cloth and tied it around her head which held back her naturally spiraling hair. It had grown in length and could now be stretched down to touch her shoulders before it sprang back to halo her head. She had placed a bit of makeup on for no other reason then when she looked in the mirror, she actually liked what she saw, and knew she could like it even more with some lip-gloss and eye shadow.

When Dani answered her door, her mouth actually dropped.

"Hayden, you look... terrific!" Her friend grabbed her arm and led her inside. "Girl, Sean is going to love you!"

Out on the patio, Dante was standing with an extremely handsome man, and both were drinking beers. Dante did a double take and nearly dropped his.

"Hayden?"

"Hey Dante."

"Wow, you lost a lot of weight!" Dani smacked his arm until his mouth clamped shut. Dante was attractive, built like a wrestler with light skin and eyes. He was also a little immature but despite their numerous problems, Dani thought he was too cute to let go. It was a mentality she understood well because it was exactly how she used to feel about MyKell.

The man standing next to Dante was on a whole different level though. He could have modeled men's underwear with his tall, toned body. When Dani said that he was dark, she hadn't lied. Sean was Morris Chestnut dark and he towered over her at well over 6′3″ or maybe 6′4″ – at the least. To say that he was handsome was an understatement. Dani had not exaggerated.

Sean's brow lifted and he took her hand and shook it slightly. "Hi Hayden. I've heard a great deal about you. I'm Sean. Sean Crosley."

"I've heard a great deal about you too." She smiled. Strangely, she felt very relaxed and at ease. Back in the day, meeting a guy on a blind date was stressful and hellacious, and if he was good-looking, she was sure to make a total fool out of herself. Yet the conversation was easy, perhaps because although Sean was attractive, she wasn't attracted to him. He was nice, attentive, smart and very good-looking, but her mind was on someone else.

Hayden was having a nice time and the steaks were perfect. Yet she couldn't stop her mind from drifting. She wished that she could find a polite way to make a get-away and then she felt guilty about her anti-social attitude. It was at that moment that her cell phone vibrated and announced that a text message had been received – right in the middle of a funny story that Sean was telling.

She quickly apologized and then moved away to read the message. It was from Brian announcing that he was at the grocery store and was unsure about what kind of oatmeal to buy. Her heartbeat began to race and a smile spread across her face.

"Why in the world do we need oatmeal for meatloaf and smothered cabbage?" he texted.

"We need it to hold the meatloaf together and to keep it moist. Don't forget eggs."

"Got that. Would you like something to drink; diet cola? Wine?"

"Wine would be nice. It's not really on my diet… but one glass of Moscato won't hurt."

"Moscato it is. So I see they have all kinds of oatmeal here."

"Do not get the instant kind. It has sugar in it."

"Lol! Okay honey, I do know that much."

She smiled and then remembered that she was supposed to be trying to get to know a man that didn't interest her half as much as the one she was texting.

"I'm sorry, I have to go. Hanging out with friends."
"Okay, have fun beautiful. See you tomorrow."
"Can't wait."

She quickly returned to the party, wiping the smile of pleasure from her face. A short time later, Dani whisked her away to help her with some manufactured task in the kitchen. Her friend was beaming.

"I really think Sean likes you! Isn't he terrific?"

Hayden nodded. "He's nice." She grabbed a dish of chocolate mousse. "Grab something so it doesn't look so obvious that we're in here comparing notes."

Dani gave her a look of disbelief. "Oh come on... you like him right?"

Hayden shrugged again before walking out the room. "Not as much as you do."

"Hayden!" Dani whispered loudly but Hayden didn't stop walking until she was back out on the patio. She didn't stay much longer after that, apologizing for being exhausted after a long week and today's additional hours at work. She was truly tired but mostly tired of faking interest in a man that Dani obviously had a crush on.

"Maybe we'll see each other again?" Sean asked while taking her hand. For a moment she thought he was going to kiss it. She gave him a smile.

"Nice meeting you Sean." No promises, no lies.

Hayden heard the alarm clock and her heart sank. *I can't get up. I can't go to the park today. I can't.*

"'I am perfectly imperfect...'" Hayden muttered tiredly. "'I strive for better while loving all that I am today.'" She forced her eyes to open. "'In loving myself today, I am better equipped to improve myself tomorrow. Now get your ass up Hayden!'"

Hayden sat up and dragged herself to the edge of the bed where she sat for another minute until she was awake enough to stumble into the bathroom. She was at the park right at 8:00 A.M. just as she would have been if Todd and Kevin were coming along.

"Hi Miss Hayden!" She turned quickly to the familiar voice and smiled genuinely when she saw Kevin getting out of a car.

"Kevin – you came!"

"Yep, my mom drove me." He ran over to Hayden then and accepted a brief hug. Now a woman was getting out of her car, along with another little boy who appeared to be about six or seven; Kevin's brother Adrian. Hayden looked at the smiling face of Todd's wife – Kia.

"Hi. So I finally get to meet you," Kia said before they shook hands. Hayden didn't know if she had expected a light-skinned woman with long hair and a model body, but Kia wasn't that at all. She was full-figured and curvy, but toned in a way that reminded her of tennis star Serena Williams. Kia's short-cropped hair framed a deep nut-brown face and she had a natural beauty that had no need of makeup.

"It's nice to meet you Kia." Then Hayden looked at the smaller guy that watched her curiously. "And you must be Adrian."

He nodded shyly.

"Todd said you'd be here and I didn't want Kevin to miss any training days." Kia chuckled. "I hope you don't mind that I brought him because I don't do the jogging thing," which was evidenced by her attire of sandals and a sundress.

"I can't miss a training day either if I expect to run a fifty-K in a few months. These few months are definitely not enough time to become a marathon runner."

Kia gave her a polite once over. "Todd says you'll be able to do it. He's really proud of your accomplishments. You're lucky because you have a runner's body; compact with long legs."

Hayden's brow went up. Runner's body? Yeah, right! Not with all this lose skin beneath her clothes...

Kia smiled and then covered her mouth and tried to stop. "I'm so sorry; it's just that Todd told me how much you hate compliments."

Hayden chuckled. "I'm that obvious?"

Kia shook her head and Kevin interrupted. "Mom! You're taking us off schedule," he said impatiently.

"Kevin. Patience." Her attention returned to Hayden. "Todd says that you could be a personal trainer." Hayden had never considered that before; her a personal trainer? She could be one though, couldn't she?

"So as my son has so rudely reminded me, I should let you guys get back on schedule."

"We'll be back in about an hour."

"Mama, can I get on the swings now?" the little guy asked.

She took his hand. "Yes. Have a good run guys."

As Hayden led Kevin across the street to the jogging trail, she found herself liking Kia and wondering if it would be improper to ask her questions about interracial dating. Hayden wanted to know how being of different races affected her and Todd's relationship. Hayden had never dated outside of her race and knew that there was still racism in society.

In this day and age, people of almost all colors used "the N-word" fondly, even in pop culture. Hate crimes continued, bad cops still targeted minorities, and the court system perpetrated racial inequality. Hayden didn't usually think much about race, although she was probably guilty of having made some stupid racially insensitive comment at some point or another. It was all a lot to think about.

As Hayden and Kevin jogged, she wondered how she would react to people making such comments about Whites now that she was romantically interested in a White man. If someone made the comment, "Just like a White person..." would she respond by saying, "I know! My *White* boyfriend does that all the time!" She giggled to herself and Kevin gave her a curious look.

"Miss Hayden, you're running faster than Dad—I mean Todd!"

She slowed their pace, realizing that she had been the one setting their speed. "I thought I was following you!"

"No, I was following you!"

"You're killing me Kevin..." she panted, and then they giggled.

~Chapter 13~
THE YEAR THAT HAD NEVER BEEN THROWN AWAY

Hayden returned home to shower and to change for both work and her dinner with Brian later that evening. As she showered, she allowed her hands to run down over her rolls of flesh and loose skin. She thought about what Kia had said; that she had a runner's body; compact with long legs. Yet she still felt and looked like she always had, just a smaller fat woman...

When she got out the shower she walked naked into her bedroom and stood in front of the full-length mirror that hung on the back of her bedroom door. When she hated herself, she couldn't see herself, even when she glanced at a mirror, put on makeup, or washed her face.

So while Hayden no longer hated herself, she had not regained the ability to look in the mirror and to see what was right in front of her. She only saw a fat woman with sagging breasts and a belly that had flesh which could be pulled up and down like an apron! She took in a shaky breath and closed her eyes. "I am going to look at a woman that has a runner's body; compact with long legs..."

She slowly opened her eyes and looked at the body — not her face, just *her* body. She gasped. Her waist curved inward and then swelled out towards hips that swelled perfectly. Her breasts sat on her chest but her nipples tipped upward quite full and not pendulous the way she had imagined. Her stomach protruded some below her belly button but she could only grip it if she pulled and stretched the skin there.

Hayden's eyes scanned down to legs and thighs that were toned and... were those muscles in the front of her thighs? She studied her calves and saw that they were rock hard. Hayden lifted her arms and made a muscle. She jiggled them and nothing swayed like a turkey neck!

She allowed her eyes to scan her face. Big brown eyes stared back at her and she wondered if they always looked like this; as if her soul was wide open and all of her secrets were spilling out. She ran her hands through her thick hair and watched it spring back into place; spirals framing her face as if she had purchased a wig—but this was all hers, thick, natural, spiraling curls.

Hayden sank down onto the edge of her bed allowing big hot tears to roll down her cheeks and splash her bare knees. That woman in the mirror was her? Why had she only seen the other woman that she once was in her mind's eye? Even when people told her otherwise, she had still never seen anything but the other Hayden; the one that she would never, ever allow to come back to fill her with doubt and self-hate.

After a moment, she took several deep, cleansing breaths. After dressing in another sundress, this one barely reaching her knees, Hayden went down into her kitchen and looked at the calendar. It was the end of September. In just over two weeks, it would literally be six months since she had made a vow to get right with herself.

She took down the calendar and stared at it. It was scribbled on with affirmations and notes and reminders. She had never thrown away a year of her life—she had been living it all along.

When Hayden finally walked into the office, Brian looked up from his desk, a look of relief on his face. He jumped up and came over to her, but then stopped at the sight of her in a pretty dress and low heels. He just stared until Hayden began to fidget uncomfortably before he shook his head and smiled.

"Is... everything okay?" she asked nervously.

"Uh... what?" he asked, distractedly, eyes still glued onto her.

Pam let out a disgusted sigh. "Brine, cat got your tongue? Tell her she looks nice."

"You do!" he said and she took her seat relieved and a teeny bit thrilled.

"I was just worried because it was after twelve and... well I was thinking you'd be in at eight and then we could... uh, eat at around noon."

"I'm sorry Brian! I jogged this morning and spent a bit too much time getting ready for... dinner tonight."

The mere mention of dinner was causing her to tingle. She hoped her eyes weren't revealing her thoughts, so she quickly began straightening her already neat desk so that she wouldn't expose those private thoughts.

"No, it's fine. I just... wanted you to have time to relax as well as eat."

"Then she should probably get to work..." Pam said while coming to her feet and heading to the canteen with her pack of cigarettes. She winked at Hayden on her way out.

"Right! Oh, and I have a surprise for you too! But I'll tell you about that later on." He was smiling mysteriously now.

"A secret. Ugh... I'm not good with secrets."

"Well, this is a good one."

"Uh... that's even worse. Anticipation is like — pressure and anxiety-"

"Okay, I'll tell you," he interrupted. "You won the bonus!"

"The year's worth of free gasoline?" Her voice was sharp with excitement. "Ooh! I needed that!"

Brian was grinning brightly. "Okay, you'll have to pretend to be surprised Monday because Dad wanted to make an official announcement."

She nodded quickly. "Oh I won't have to pretend. This is going to make me geeked for the next three months!"

The workday moved slowly and Hayden was tired, not even the lure of Brian, eating, relaxing and kissing could abate her exhaustion. She had to mask it though, or Brian might cancel. So she went into the canteen for a Coca Cola. It would be her first soda in months, but she needed the caffeine.

Abdullah was standing by the microwave waiting for his smelly lunch to warm. She looked over at him as she slipped her dollar bill into the vending machine. She retrieved the soda and then walked over to her co-worker.

"What are you eating Abdullah?"

"Goat curry and Babba Ghannouj Hayden."

"Babba Ghannouj... are you Turkish?"

He shrugged. "Kurdish."

"Ah." Well no wonder she couldn't figure out his racial background. She knew nothing about Kurdish people. She stifled a yawn.

"Are you okay? You look tired. We've all been working quite hard this week." The microwave sounded and he opened it allowing the aroma of his meal to fill the area. He carefully retrieved the bubbling dish leaving a trail of something that looked like rice but wasn't, along with splatters of liquid.

She sighed. "I'm fine. I just came in for a soda to pick me up."

"I have Turkish coffee in my thermos. My wife makes it and people actually give her money to make it for them each morning."

She was interested because she'd never had Turkish coffee, but didn't think she could drink anything that was in Abdullah's thermos.

"I usually drink it after my meal, but you're welcome to it. There is more at home."

She nodded and smiled. "Thank you Abdullah." Then she paused. "Abdullah, I wanted to ask you about something..."

He put his hot food on the table leaving another trail.

"Yes Hayden?"

"Why don't you cover your food when you heat it?"

"Uh... what?"

She smiled. "Abdullah, would you mind cleaning up your spills?"

He looked at her in surprise; maybe because she was smiling at him while criticizing him, therefore he wasn't sure how to take it.

He pursed his lips together. "Fine!" he snapped. "But I think I'll just drink my own Turkish coffee!"

She nodded once and then left.

Later when he passed her desk to return to work, he muttered something under his breath. However, a minute later he carried a thermos and two small carryout cups.

"Our coffee is very strong, like our people. A small amount is all you need." He poured them each a cup of the thick hot liquid. She hid a grimace thinking that it would be extremely bitter, but on the contrary, it was slightly sweet and reminded her of a mocha coffee. She drained her cup in three swallows and then nodded and smiled.

"It was delicious Abdullah. I've never had anything like it."

He gave her a pleased look before returning to his desk.

It was nearly 5:00 P.M. before Hayden had put in her four hours. The coffee had done wonders. When she gathered her things and met Brian at the door, she was full of energy and thought she could probably jog around the building.

"Hey beautiful."

"Hi."

"I don't live too far from here. You can follow me or we can ride over together and I'll bring you back to your car later."

She agreed to allow him to drive and as soon as they were in the car Brian leaned over and kissed her lips gently.

"I've been thinking about that for days."

She touched his face. "Me too." This time, she kissed him, but only briefly and then she pulled back. He started the car seemingly very content.

Hayden was happy that Brian had offered to drive because he lived in a portion of Villa Hills, Kentucky that she wasn't familiar with and though it only took 15 minutes, they drove through several winding streets.

"I can't wait to see how you make something like cabbage even remotely desirable," he said.

"Honey, if you fry anything with bacon and onions, it's a given that it will be good."

"Hmmm." He pulled up to a duplex that overlooked the hills leading to the Ohio River.

"This is pretty," she said as he opened the car door for her.

"It's a great place to watch the fireworks."

He took her hand and led her to his apartment. It was an open concept room with a staircase leading up to the second level. It was minimally decorated with black leather furniture and chrome finishes, a sharp contrast to the white carpeting and white walls. Normally she wouldn't have liked it, but the splashes of deep red and neon blue gave the room life.

She turned and smiled at him. "I love your place." He had been staring at her and he quickly blushed.

"I'll take you on a tour after we get dinner started." He still held her hand and led her to the kitchen.

"This is... *wow!*"

He had all stainless steel appliances, an island, and the dark cabinetry looked great with sea green mosaic tile.

"I don't use it much, well other than the microwave." He grabbed two bottles of Moscato but different brands. "Which one?" She pointed to the Barefoot Bubbly and then he poured them two wine glasses full.

She closed her eyes in pleasure as the cold fluid hit her liquor-deprived senses.

"This is so good." She felt him close and when she opened her eyes Brian's lips were inches from hers. Instead of kissing her like she expected, he took the glass from her and placed it on the bar and then he nipped her lips lightly.

His hands captured her waist and he pulled her close to him. "Hayden..."

Her arms wrapped themselves around his neck and she allowed her body to mold against his. Before she knew it, they were kissing wildly and her leg had moved to wrap around his waist.

He clutched her thigh, allowing his hand to glide upward where he grabbed her ass. She felt him inhale a shaky breath before his hands began gripping and kneading her flesh. She felt him growing hard against her pelvis and with her dress hiked up and her leg around him his grinding hips pushed against places that even she hadn't touched in ages.

Electrical shocks traveled up her body and her eyes began to blink at the rapid onslaught of pleasure. Brian groaned and turned her slightly so that her back was against the cabinet. His hips began to thrust against her rapidly and Hayden's fist buried into the length of hair at the back of his neck.

He swiftly lifted her and she wrapped both her legs around him. Brian pulled back slightly, never breaking the connection between their rapidly pumping and rolling hips. He sat her rump on the cabinet and then clutched her breast. He sought her nipple through the material of her bra and pinched and rubbed it until he caused it to thicken and poke against the material.

She cried out in pleasure, feeling the juices slipping from her opening and wanted more than anything to rip off her damp panties and to feel him against her, skin-to-skin.

"Please Brian!" she whimpered her need.

"*God*, Hayden!" Then he reached between them and released himself from his pants. She didn't bother to look; she wantonly spread her legs as she sought his lips and tongue. A moment later, his fingers had pulled aside the damp crotch of her panties, and then she felt something big and slick separating her swollen flesh just before it pushed into her.

Her breath died in her chest for one tortuous moment and when it returned, she wailed and thrust frantically against him, feeling the stretch that was just this side of pain and much more

114

that side of amazing. She could not think, or attempt to control her movements and sounds. All she knew was that the pistoning of Brian's hips could not end — not until...

"*Brian!*" she screamed as her body trembled uncontrollably until there were mini quakes overtaking her.

At the sound of her climax, Brian pulled the fabric at the top of her dress downward, along with her strapless bra, until her left breast tumbled free. His mouth immediately clamped onto her swollen nipple and he sucked and worked it as he rapidly thrust in and out of her tight opening. Hayden's hands became claws as she gripped and held onto him, while her orgasm slashed through her violently.

Her uncontrolled spasms gripped and milked him until his control was shattered and with a guttural groan he fired shots of his semen repeatedly into her depths. Hayden was unsure how long that had all lasted, it could have been seconds, it could have been an hour, but what she did know was that she had never experienced anything like it. She had no idea that she could experience such a level of pleasure. MyKell hadn't been her only lover, there had been a few others before him, but nothing had come close to the place that Brian had just taken her.

Brian pulled out of her and then leaned his forehead against her chest while he caught his breath. She stroked his hair thinking that this was the most perfect moment. People always said to find her perfect place, and she knew that this moment in time would be hers.

Brian raised his head; his eyes were worried when they met hers. "Hayden..." He still hadn't fully caught his breath, but the expression on his face was nowhere near as happy as hers.

"We should not have done that," he said softly.

Her eyes widened in surprise. He shook his head and quickly kissed her lightly on the lips. "No, not that! *That* was beautiful honey. But we didn't use protection-"

She placed her palms gently on his cheeks. "It's okay. I've been on the pill since I was a teenager. It helps to keep my cycle regular."

He didn't seem relieved by that explanation. After inhaling deeply, he stared into her eyes. "Honey... I don't have unprotected sex. Not ever. This is the first time that I've ever done that."

"Ever?"

"Ever." He frowned and lightly gnawed his lip. "It was... amazing." He quickly kissed her and then stared into her eyes again as if something worried him.

She waited, confused about his mix signals.

"You know that I've used heroin-"

Her back suddenly stiffened and she looked like she was about to hyperventilate. He clutched her arms firmly then, but not painfully.

"No! I'm not HIV positive and I don't have any STDs. I get tested twice a year."

"You've shared needles?" she asked in a weak voice. What was wrong with her? Why hadn't she realized this? All she'd considered was her inability to get pregnant, but she had never even bothered to ask about his health before taking this step.

"Hayden, listen to me. I'm clean. I don't have anything. But you and I have to be careful. I want to be inside of you as often as possible; but not without protection. Not until I'm satisfied that there is not going to be anything... to worry about."

He stared at her, searching her face for her acceptance or rejection.

After a moment her racing heartbeat slowed. "Brian, I understand. You're clean. You don't have anything... but you could have."

He nodded, seeming relieved that she understood what bothered him.

"I wouldn't put some random woman at risk, so I sure as hell won't put you at risk. And as much as saying this makes me want to choke, if you do... make love with someone other than me, then I don't want you to put yourself at risk with them, either."

She nodded in understanding and then placed her arms around his neck and then they touched foreheads.

"Hayden?"

"Hmmm?"

"We have to cook on this counter so... maybe you should get down."

She made a face and punched him lightly on the arm.

He laughed and picked her up before he set her lightly on her feet, but not before thoroughly exploring her mouth with his again.

~Chapter 14~
A RIPPLE IN THE WATER AND THE SMELL OF MORNING SEX

Dinner was exquisite, even though it was just chicken wings from a carryout pizza place. Neither of them had felt in the mood to prepare and wait for meatloaf and cabbage. Besides, there really wasn't much time since they moved to the bedroom and spent several hours there making love instead.

Hayden was nuzzled against Brian's chest. He stroked the fine hairs along her temple and she relaxed even more. She didn't feel self-conscious being naked in front of him. He was turned on by her and that turned her on. Besides, she was content to watch him equally as naked.

"Brian?"

"Hmm?"

"Why did you stare at me that first day? When I first showed up at the office?"

His hand paused and she looked up at him and waited.

"Oh…" He smiled without saying more and she propped herself up on her arm, looking at him and continuing to wait patiently.

He sighed. "That wasn't the first time I'd seen you," he finally confessed.

She frowned. "You'd seen me before? When?"

He looked down and gave her a wry smile. "I'm not a stalker, okay? But it might sound like I am."

"Gotcha," she waited now very curious.

118

"This last time that I returned to the office, my dad and I had an agreement that I wouldn't leave the building during work hours. So smoking and eating and anything else had to be done within an eight point five hour time period and within the office only. I'm not... complaining.

"I had messed up pretty badly the last time I was there. I had gotten out of rehab and went right back on heroin. I would leave the office, meet my dealer and do basically what Marcus used to do; get high in the parking lot or restroom." His playful look disappeared as he watched her seriously. "We haven't talked about this part of my life, but when I came back this last time, it was after going cold turkey off heroin."

"Jesus Brian... isn't that dangerous?"

"Well, I'd just been through rehab, so my body had already gone through a break from the drug. But yes, it was dangerous, and I sure didn't feel as if I'd survive it. Anyway Hayden, that part is a horrible story and I'll tell you about it some other time, but not right now. So when I returned to work, it was about a month after I'd quit and I was still pretty sick."

Hayden recalled how skinny and pale he was back then. Heroin withdrawal... damn, it made her feel sad for him. She glanced down at his forearm where the flesh was mottled and scarred from repeated needle injections. Hayden moved back into his arms and he cuddled her while continuing his story.

"In the beginning, I really needed to smoke; the nicotine just helped. But thinking about that canteen was bad. My system was already screwy and my stomach couldn't take the smell of Abdullah's food or the sight of everything else going on in there."

Hayden huffed her agreement.

"I wasn't used to it, the way the rest of them were, because when I worked in Lexington, my employees didn't live like that. But that first day when I went in for a smoke, I saw that the canteen was clean. I mean, I could smell the disinfectant and just the smell of something clean helped to keep me from being nauseous. I'm sorry to say that I didn't really think too much more about it. But then one day when I was leaving, I noticed a woman sitting in her car, looking annoyed."

Hayden lifted her brow at him.

"I figured this woman was waiting to give one of the other employees a ride home, but to my surprise, she went into the office once everyone was gone and being curious, I waited for her to leave to see if she would come out carrying some computers or something."

Hayden made a face at him and he gave her a wry grin.

"Well, she wasn't carrying anything and I went home no longer curious."

"You thought I was a burglar with my own key?"

"I thought you were a very well-dressed cleaning lady." He leaned over and kissed her. "A very sexy, well-dressed cleaning lady."

"Yeah, right."

"A couple of weeks later, when you came into the office during work hours, I knew I'd seen you before, but I wasn't sure where. I was trying to figure it out." He shrugged.

"I thought something was wrong with you," Hayden confessed.

"There was." He chuckled. "But I was somewhat preoccupied at that time."

Hayden looked down at his hand and then intertwined their fingers.

"You make me happy Hayden."

Instead of asking why, she just smiled.

"Sweetheart. It's time to wake up."

Hayden's eyes popped open and she nearly jumped straight out of her skin at the whispered words and brush of lips against her ear. She looked around frantically and Brian kissed her neck.

"Shhh," he whispered. "It's okay. You're still at my house."

"Oh my God! Brian, what time is it?"

"It's just before five am."

Hayden tried to process that. 5:00 A.M. What did that mean? It meant that she'd slept in Brian's bed all night!

"I have to get to work-"

"Mmm hmm…" Brian agreed slowly and lazily. His lips were still very close to her neck. "You're going to put on a pair of my sweat pants and a t-shirt, we're going to make you some oatmeal; I happen to have two types because I didn't know the best one to get for meatloaf. Then I'm going to drive you to your car. You're going to drive to the gym, workout and then go back to your house to get ready for the day."

Hayden relaxed as she realized that it was a good plan. Then she still gave him an accusing look. "You didn't wake me up."

"You needed the sleep. I told you that I intended for you to get some rest. Plus, I admit that I enjoyed the company… despite the snoring."

She huffed. "I know I snore! It used to make MyKell…" She blinked at the way his name just slid from her lips. "He used to complain about it."

"Well, I won't be complaining. The sound of it was like a lullaby. It helped me to fall asleep."

She squinted at him. "You are one strange man Brian Fox. But I like it." She smiled and kissed him and then prepared to get out of his bed. "Ugh, I smell like… sex in the morning!"

Brian placed his hand on her leg. "No you don't. But you will…"

Hayden looked down at the bed sheet covering his lower body. *Oh my…* There was a tent there. Any thoughts of sleep, work, the gym or leaving immediately all disappeared.

Boldly, she slipped the sheet from Brian's body and marveled at his solid form. She didn't want to think of MyKell, but couldn't help compare the two. There was at least a 10-year difference in age between both men, and it was obvious in the hard lines of Brian's muscles.

Her eyes hungrily scoured his perfectly toned body. Once upon a time, she had thought he was too thin. Yet not when she looked at him lying in bed with one arm under his head, and one knee bent just so in order to frame the sight of a thick and throbbing penis surrounded by sandy colored pubic hair. A trail of light colored hair traveled from the thick thatch of his pelvis, and then meandered around his belly button where it then spread lightly across his toned chest.

Her eyes moved to his face where his lips were slightly tilted up in a wicked smile, and this time Hayden knew that she was being thoroughly seduced by this man. Grey eyes captured and trapped her, freezing her like a deer caught in the headlights. His tousled hair falling into his face and the soft stubble across his normally clean-shaven face completed an erotic picture that brought her body to life, her pussy weeping with need. She slipped back into bed and straddled his hips, rising up on her knees enough to rock them back and forth until she bumped his cock and caused it to rock forward. Brian caught his breath and then moved his hands to roam up her bare thighs.

"Ride me Hayden."

She braced herself on his forearms, the tips of her fingers brushing against the mottled skin of his old track marks. She traced each mark, each ripple of flesh until she felt him shiver and goose bumps began to rise beneath her fingers. When she met his eyes, he watched her with a speculative look on his face and in embarrassment, she moved her hand.

"No," he stopped her. "Nobody has ever done that before. I like it."

As she resumed her exploration of his old scars, he raised his hands and cupped her breasts. His fingers began to caress her nipples and Hayden's rocking hips intensified into a fast grind. Having him touch her there with so much care and desire was her undoing. To be touched so intimately while his cock bobbed in front of her was a sensual and visual stimulant. She wondered how simple touching could make her want to come and scream it to the world?

Hayden suddenly gasped and her rolling hips became staccato. "Brian!" He reached over and grasped a condom from the bedside table, which he quickly ripped open. The condom went on half a second before Hayden gripped his shaft, angling the head of his cock to her rapidly pulsating opening. He thrust forward and slipped inside of her one breath later and the pain and pleasure combination only intensified her orgasm.

Spasms gripped and held him within her depths, milking at his engorged shaft while his pelvis rose and fell rhythmically against her. Her body bounced with each hard thrust. It felt so good! He was bigger than MyKell and the newness of an act that she hadn't engaged in during the last few months, as well as his much bigger and harder size, reached places that sent her mind flying in a million different directions.

She cried out a ragged screech at her prolonged climax. Never before had she been so out of control that she couldn't end the explosions within her depths. She quaked, screamed and grabbed him blindly as he rapidly thrust in and out of her — only released from her torturous orgasm after he yelled his own release.

Bucking frantically, he gripped her hips, holding her in place until he somehow swapped their positions, and now lay on top of her body buried balls deep inside of her. His body trembled as he ejaculated all that remained in his testicles, down to the last drop. When she could again think, Hayden stared up at the ceiling while Brian lay gasping for breath next to her, his hand gently stroking her inner thigh. She smiled feeling loved and accepted and thought of her very own affirmation.

I am surrounded by love and everything is fine.

Hayden was still smiling when she drove to her first job on Monday morning. She had gotten in her hour workout and was still able to make it into work by 8:00 A.M., and that was despite Brian's promise to make her smell like morning sex. She couldn't believe it when she began tingling down low at just the memory of it. How was that possible? She had just had sex five and a half times in the last 24 hours. It would have been six had she not fallen asleep the night before when Brian was beginning some thoroughly relaxing foreplay.

Dani was grinning too when she walked over to Hayden's desk. "Girl, you aren't mad at me, are you?"

"Mad at you about what?" Hayden asked in a raspy voice due to strained vocal chords caused by screaming out during her morning orgasm.

"Uh, what in the world is wrong with your voice?"

Hayden touched her throat quickly. "Uh..."

"Hayden! Did you do the nasty?" Hayden shushed her and looked around quickly. "We are going to talk about this at break," Dani said as she quickly sauntered back to her workstation.

"What-?" She wanted to ask what she should be mad about, but let it drop for now. Ugh, Hayden wished that she had some hot tea for her throat. Yet, she smiled immediately as she remembered why her throat was so sore.

At break, Dani gave her a sheepish smile. "So you're not mad?"

"*About what?*"

"Uh... don't you check your phone messages? I sorta gave Sean your phone number and he sent you a text—don't be mad, don't be mad! I promise I'm not trying to sabotage you and Brian, even though it might appear that way-"

Hayden dug her phone out of her purse, but it was dead. "I have to charge it."

"He left the message Saturday night while he was still at our house. You haven't checked your phone since then?"

Hayden rolled her eyes. "I was a little preoccupied." She grimaced at her friend. "Why would you give Sean my phone number?"

"Honestly, it was because he said he thoroughly enjoyed your company and wanted to tell you himself."

"Hmph," Hayden replied. It was annoying, but she was on cloud nine and nothing was going to deflate her bubble. "Well, I will be sure to let you know what the message says once I charge my phone."

"I have a charger at my desk, I'll give it to you and then you can tell me at lunch. But don't worry, I can tell by the fact that your voice is gone and your face is all pink that you had a pretty good time with Brian. So... I'll butt out. I promise."

Hayden touched her face and blushed even further. Hayden was more anxious about missing texts from Brian than she cared about what Sean had to say, but Sean's text was front and center after she had borrowed her nosey friend's charger and was able to read her messages again.

"Hello Hayden. Danyelle gave me your number because I wanted to send you a message letting you know how much I enjoyed meeting you Saturday. If you are interested I have tickets to the Fiery Foods Show at the convention center and would like to get to know you better. Hope to hear from you soon. Sean."

Dani squealed in excitement when Hayden read the message to her. "So what are you going to tell him?"

"I'm not going to tell him anything—you are. You can start by apologizing for giving him my number when I'm already in a relationship and then you can go to the fiery foods show with him yourself. Though first, I'd advise you to dump Dante."

Dani's mouth dropped open, but Hayden held up her hand.

"Just tell him how you feel about him Danyelle. Because once you put it out there, then there are no more games, no questions— you'll know whether you need to drop it and move on, or whether there's something there that might turn into something beautiful."

"But... he's Dante's friend..."

"Dante who?"

Dani chuckled. "That's cold."

Hayden shook her head adamantly. "It's necessary. If you find yourself disliking him more than you like him, then you can either try to fix it or just walk away. You think I don't know that it's easier said than done?

"But now that MyKell is out off my life, I feel so much peace. I don't wake up annoyed, thinking that a deadbeat is lying next to me, or wondering how long before he quits his latest job, or gets fired. I don't have to wonder if I'm annoying him as much as he's annoying me. It's done now, and I'm at peace with it."

Dani nodded. "You're right. We've just been together for so long and I do love him but… I'm not in love with Dante anymore. He's cheated and he takes me for granted." Dani sighed. "I would like to be in love again. If not with Dante, then with someone who wants it just as much as I do."

"Good girl."

Hayden's heart was pumping wildly when she walked into Fox Vinyl. She immediately looked over to where Brian was currently sitting and he was already watching the door for her. They both grinned like idiots when they saw each other.

He had indeed been texting her and had become worried when she hadn't responded. After explaining her forgotten charger, they spent the rest of the afternoon texting — well actually, it was called *sexting*. When she saw his latest text, Hayden suppressed the naughty giggle that wanted to force its way from her mouth.

Brian was very good at reminding her of all the things they had done the night before, as well as that morning, and how mutually enjoyable it had been. Eventually, he came over to her desk, she assumed to pick up his dinner. Instead, he leaned down and kissed her lightly on the lips.

"How is my woman this evening?"

She gave him a look of surprise, first since he had kissed her publicly, but second, because he had so clearly established that she was his. They hadn't talked about it, but it was pretty obvious that neither was in it for a casual fling. However, it must still be a man thing because Brian had certainly gathered everyone's attention as he broadcast his claim on her.

"Uh… your woman is fine. And how is my man?" That statement sent a nice tingle up her spine.

His brow quirked up at the sound of her hoarse voice and then he straightened proudly and whispered, "Wishing you would come over tonight."

Hayden laughed lightly and looked around at their co-workers who watched them with open curiosity or surprise.

"Brian," she whispered. "I can't during the week-"

"Sure you can. Just pack an overnight bag. Didn't we make it work today?"

She paused. "Yeah, but you live in Kentucky and I live five minutes from my gym-"

He hid a grin and looked up into the air as if in deep thought. "So true... hmmm I wonder how we can work that out with me doing all the moving in the morning and you going straight in to workout..."

Abdullah stood up. "*Rahimullah* Hayden! You really don't take hints well."

Hayden shot Abdullah an embarrassed look as she realized that even if she whispered in a room full of nosey people, they could still hear everything that she said. "Hush you!" She looked at Pam ready to tell her the same thing, but the older woman raised her hands innocently. Hayden's eyes met Brian's again and his face was red, with him nearly bursting from the desire to laugh.

Hayden shook her head. "I was just getting ready to invite you to my house before Mr. Buttinsky interrupted. And contrary to what *some other people think*, I do know how to take hints," she lied. "Now, if you will follow me home this evening, I believe that would be the best solution."

Brian's arms were crossed before him and he was hiding his mouth as he nodded his agreement, but she knew he was still trying not to laugh.

"I *can* take a hint," she exclaimed.

Abdullah made a choking, laughing sound that he tried to hide behind a cough. He then quickly picked up his phone and began fake dialing... as if she hadn't done that herself a time or two...

127

"You are too cute sweetheart. Now give me a smile."

She tried to resist, but he just had it like that.

"Come on, we have time to eat in the canteen. Plus I want to show you something." He grabbed their lunch and she followed him to the canteen to eat with him for the first time in over a week.

Hayden halted before entering, and Brian turned and looked at her with a smile. Hayden blinked. The room was actually clean!

There was a hand written sign taped to the shelf above the microwave which stated: "CLEAN YOUR OWN MESS." There were two large garbage tubs on either side of the door and a new paper towel dispenser suspended on the wall.

"Whoa, what happened in here?" she asked as she spun in a slow circle.

"Abdullah did this."

"*What?* Abdullah?"

"Yeah, he was cleaning the microwave this morning and cursing up a blue streak. Someone began to applaud and then soon everyone had come in applauding and saying that it was about time."

Brian set their food on one of the tables. "He got so pissed that he left. I figured he went home for the day, but he was back an hour later with all this stuff. And then someone left spilled coffee in the microwave and he went back to his desk and wrote that sign."

Hayden thought back to her words to him on Friday. She thought about the time she had apologized to him even though she was the one that he'd yelled at. It was like ripples in the water. She had caused the first ripple and its effect was continuing to move.

~Chapter 15~
A PERSON BENEATH ME CAN'T HURT ME

Hayden was anxious when Brian stepped into her house, but it was clean even if she had neglected her weekly dusting. Brian was quiet as he looked around, walking from room to room on the first level until they ended up in the kitchen.

He turned to her. "This is you Hayden." He was nodding his head. "This place feels like you."

"It does?"

"It's comfortable, pretty and it makes me want to relax."

She hugged him. "Thank you."

The two lovers showered together and at first, Hayden didn't want Brian to wash her when he offered. Then she realized that it was what he wanted. She watched him run the soapy sponge across her body and as his penis grew in size, she forgot about any of her physical imperfections, like stretch marks and loose skin. She was attracted to Brian and not at all affected by his scarred forearms. S why wouldn't it be the same for him?

Brian wouldn't let Hayden dry herself. After he patted her skin with a towel, he led her to the bedroom where he had her lay on the bed. He spread her light brown legs and then kissed her moist nether lips until she writhed and moaned and then climaxed for the first, but not the last time tonight.

Hours later, although she should have been sleeping, Hayden lay wrapped in Brian's arms, wide awake and deep in thought.

"Are you still awake?" she whispered.

"No."

Hayden smiled and Brian turned to kiss her forehead. "I like sleeping with you in my arms Hayden."

"I like it too."

"Then why aren't you sleeping?"

"Why aren't you?"

"Because you woke me up." He yawned and then nuzzled her neck. "My woman need some more loving?" She felt him slowly harden against her thigh.

"I... well..." How could she say no when he was so delicious?

He lifted his head and met her eyes seriously. "What's wrong honey?"

"Everything is right. Nothing is wrong."

"Feels good, doesn't it?"

"Uh, I'm not used to the feeling."

Brian settled in against her with his lips brushing her neck. "Me neither. It's been a long time since I've felt like everything was right with the world. I think I've been on a downward spiral ever since my mother died."

Hayden relished his soft touch and she rubbed his hands that now embraced her. "You and your mom were close?"

"Yes, and my dad too. I guess I had a blessed childhood. So when Mom died, it turned my entire world upside down. And then Dad married Angela, and I couldn't understand why. She was nothing like Mom and I felt that I could see right through all her phoniness while Dad was just swept away by her looks. Hell, the first pills I ever took were the ones I stole from her purse. She was nothing but a pill popping, gold digger." Hayden was unused to hearing such angry words come from his mouth.

Hayden turned and looked down at him. "Is that why... you turned to drugs?"

He nodded, but pulled back enough to look into her eyes. "It started with Percocet and Valium. And then I was trading them in for harder stuff."

"Heroin."

"Not just heroin. Cocaine, marijuana, crystal meth. If someone said that there was a drug out there to be had, then I was going to try it."

"Wow, Brian."

He sighed. "I was just a messed up kid. But heroin turned into my drug of choice and then Percocet when I couldn't shoot up. My dad didn't really see me. He had a new life and new responsibilities. But I wasn't fooling everybody. So I asked to work in one of the other offices and Dad put me in charge of delivering the vinyl covers and collecting the money.

"I didn't start out with the intention to skim. At first, when I was flat busted broke, I borrowed the money and always put it back. But as time went on, I knew that no one else knew what I was doing, so I just started to take it. I rationalized that I was only stealing my own money since it was one day going to be my company."

Brian shook his head and sighed. Hayden turned on her side and faced him. Her hands moved up to stroke his face.

"You're telling me about a person that you used to be; a hurt and troubled man. But you aren't that person today Brian."

He watched her and a moment later, he nodded. "Well… one day, my dad came to me and he asked me point blank. He asked, but he already knew the answer and I could see it in his eyes; the disappointment, the hurt." Brian turned away and then sat up in bed.

"I need a smoke." He looked back at her and smiled. "But I'm trying to stop." He lay back down and stared at the ceiling as he thought about his words.

"I had a friend who was down on his luck. He was a hateful bastard and a bigger dope fiend than even me. But then Bill met his lady Raina and it changed him. I thought he was just a pussy so I was cool with not hanging out and getting high with him anymore.

"I went into rehab just to mollify my dad. I mean, I wasn't planning to mess up, but my heart wasn't in it. So after I got out of rehab, I just went right back to using and I hit an all time low. When Dad found out, he just washed his hands of me and turned me away.

"It hurt me so deeply...losing my Dad after everything else was too much. And I'm not blaming him or anything. It's not his fault. He hired attorneys and paid thousands for me to go away to get clean. He faced the courts all alone while I left him there to take the brunt of my mistakes. And then I come out and fuck it all up without even trying to stay straight."

Hayden reached up and lightly rubbed his back and he looked back at her with a grateful expression on his face. After a moment, he resumed his story in a much calmer voice. "When I realized that I had absolutely nothing and no one, I knew that I would end up living on the streets hustling for a fix and I wasn't going down that road. I still had too much pride and I remembered too much of the person that I was raised to be.

"So I found my friend Bill and I asked him for help. No... that's not quite true. I begged him for help. Raina only knew me as an addict, but she let me into their home and helped me while I got clean."

Hayden sat up and kissed his back. "They sound like wonderful friends."

Brian chuckled. "That's an understatement. Going cold turkey off heroin ain't no joke Hayden. It might not kill you, but it makes you want to kill yourself. I threw up so much that Bill once threatened to kick my ass if I ever even looked at a narcotic again. He said, 'If you break your freaking leg you better bite a branch and decline the drug!' And Raina was just great." He looked back at Hayden.

"She reminds me of you in some ways — but not because she's Black and lighter skinned. But there's this pain that's molded her — the same with you. She... uh..." he gestured to his face "...was burned badly as a kid so part of her face is destroyed. I think she became a certain type of person because of that injury. Just like you became a certain type of person because of yours — and me because of mine."

She blinked at his insightfulness.

"I'll introduce you two. I think you'll hit it off. Anyway, she would read to me and play music and I was hurting and cranky, but I never lashed out because everything she did helped. Everything *they* did helped.

"I lived with them for a few months until Bill kicked me out. He told me to go back home and I told him that I wasn't welcome at home. But he wouldn't let me stay, so I went back home. It was an uphill battle for a while, but I knew that Bill wasn't really kicking me out; so much as he was giving me wings. I would've never approached my dad again had he not done that."

Brian lay back down and Hayden slipped back into his arms. "I'm sorry that my life has been so fucked up. I wish that I could come to you with no history and no baggage-"

"Brian, all that's happened to you helped you to become the man that you are today. That's what you just said, right? I happen to be crazy about that man, so don't put him down. You hear me?"

He smiled. "Got it."

She kissed him.

"Thank you," he whispered.

"Why are you thanking me?"

"I'm not thanking you. I'm thanking the powers that be for creating such a wonderful woman."

She stared at him quietly. "You have such a way with words Brian Fox. I think I'm falling madly in love with you."

"Good. Now you've caught up with me."

The next morning, Brian looked tired and yawned a lot, but he moved around her kitchen comfortably, shirtless, wearing just jeans. He made her oatmeal perfectly, but wouldn't eat any, showing more interest in an old tin of coffee that he had found in the back of her fridge. Hayden loved seeing him early in the morning with tousled hair and puffy eyes. Despite his evident exhaustion, Hayden could clearly see that he enjoyed being up early with her. It didn't hurt that she sat in his lap and kissed him for a very long time before rushing to the gym for her workout with Todd.

At the gym, Todd thanked her profusely for jogging with Kevin.

She forced her mind back from thoughts of Brian. They had only managed to get worked up after their early morning make-out session. Maybe there would be time for a quickie before she left for work… She suddenly remembered to respond to Todd.

"I didn't mind at all. He's a good kid, plus I got to meet your wife. She's really nice."

Todd smiled to himself and she wondered if she should ask him about interracial dating. They had developed a true friendship over these last few months, so why not? It wasn't as if she was just being nosey, she actually felt as if she would be able to gain some perspective from someone who was going through it too.

"I've begun a relationship with someone who's a different color," she began slowly.

He looked at her with interest. "Is this your first time dating outside of your race?"

"Yes."

"Ah. Is he a White guy?"

"Yeah. Do you and Kia face any problems with issues of race?"

"No, not at all. If our families have any problems with it, then they keep their concerns to themselves. Sometimes people look, but I can't blame them for that. We're a pretty dynamic couple." He grinned.

"Kevin and Adrian's father and I had some words, but… well, that got squashed before Kia and I got married. Look, I expect that we will face some issues, but it won't make or break us, you know? For the most part, I'm not even affected by someone's racial intolerance. 'A person beneath me can't hurt me.'"

She liked that and nodded her agreement. "You are so right about that."

"Kia told me that she liked you too. She asked me to invite you over for dinner some time. You should bring your new guy."

She smiled when she thought back to when she had thought that nothing in this year would really matter. In actuality, she had found love and new friends, and most importantly of course, she had found herself.

"We'll definitely do that, thank you Todd." She slowed her treadmill down to a walk and Todd looked at her curiously.

"After the Zombie Run, I'll only be coming to the gym three times a week."

He grinned. "I think that'll be fine Hayden."

She looked ahead thoughtfully as she continued at a fast walk. "I know it seemed excessive, having to be here every single day, but..." Todd slowed his treadmill to a walk. "You weren't just working out your body; you were working out something deeper. I understood that."

She nodded and then returned her treadmill back to a jog.

To your man, you are the sun, the moon and the planet that his life orbits around. It is through those eyes that he knows the extent to which he can be loved.

Hayden read the affirmation that Brian had texted to her. It made her eyes sting that he could care as deeply for her as she did for him. It was not something she was accustomed to. In her old life, she had been grateful for just the attention of a handsome man. Yet now, someone else expressed how grateful he was for her interest. It didn't make her feel powerful or bold, but humbled that she could illicit those feelings in someone.

How was it possible that she could see this man every single day and still her heartbeat would race whenever he sent her a message on her phone, or she looked forward to the sight of him? That was easy; she had fallen deeply in love with him and that love was mutual. Brian and Hayden were nearly inseparable whenever possible; if he didn't sleep at her house, then she slept at his. Each weekend they did overtime hours together at work, and then spent the rest of the weekend enjoying each other's company.

Soon Mr. Fox decided that the company had more than caught up and they all resumed a regular work schedule. By that time, Hayden had banked several thousand dollars and in actuality, she was finally in a position to quit her second job. Except that her four hours at Fox Vinyl no longer felt like work. She enjoyed her new work team, but she couldn't continue like this forever.

Mr. Fox gave Brian much more responsibility and Hayden could see the sense of pride in her man because of it. Mr. Fox took some well-needed time off from work, leaving Brian in charge when he was out of the office. She could see that their relationship had improved tenfold. He no longer barked orders at his only son and in turn, Brian didn't seem to hate every waking second that he spent working beneath the man.

Hayden texted Brian back after reading his affirmation twice more.

"Your woman loves her man. See you tonight honey."

Todd and Kevin pulled up just then and she stowed away her cell phone and then prepared for her jog.

"Only two more weeks," Todd said.

"Me and Dad – I mean Todd!" Kevin looked embarrassed about his faux-pas. Hayden and Todd both hid smiles and pretended not to notice. He was doing it more and more often and Todd confessed that he felt torn.

He wanted to invite the boys to refer to him as their father. Yet Todd didn't want to appear to be taking over a role held by their biological father—who actually had a very good relationship with them. So the two friends spent some time thinking of nick-names like Pops, Ol' man, Daddy, etc., but Todd nixed them all. It was obvious that he just wanted to be Dad.

"Um, we found some cool costumes for the Zombie Run," Kevin continued.

"Oh yeah," Todd added. "We decided to be Team Zombie." As the trio began their slow jog, Hayden grimaced.

"I have to dress up like a zombie? I thought the runners were supposed to be chased by zombies?"

"Well… we got caught," Todd replied.

"Okay… so are we going to do all the bloody wounds?"

"Yes!" Kevin replied in excitement. "Todd stabbed some old t-shirts and put fake blood on them and then we're going to wear zombie makeup."

Hayden smiled at Kevin's youthful excitement. "I'm on board." Just two weeks until October 30th.

She wondered if she would be ready and then she stopped doubting herself. She had run a mini 10K a week ago and had finished it in mere minutes. She was ready for this. Plus she was part of a team, not by herself – Team Zombie!

Monday evening, Hayden floated into Fox Vinyl on the wings of a dove. Before she knew it she would face the marathon, and at that point she would cut her gym visits down by half, leaving her more time in the morning to cuddle and kiss. She looked forward to that, and pretty soon she would have to face another decision—it was time to quit Fox Vinyl. She hadn't discussed it with Brian, but she was tired. She wanted to do things that normal people did, like go to a movie, read a book, or just have time to stand still and do nothing.

Tomorrow would be exactly six months since she had embarked on her journey. In six months she had gained so much, but it was time to return to her life. She carried her and Brian's lunches into the canteen. It had remained clean and to keep it that way, everyone pitched in. It also helped that the current workers were those that actually weren't using the job only as a means to facilitate their next drug fix. The drug testing continued and a dress code policy of business casual work wear was instituted.

After eating, Brian gathered up their trash. "Your place or mine?"

"Mine. Tonight I want to talk about something important."

"Oh?" He quirked up a brow.

"Nothing scary." It was time to tell him that she was putting in her two weeks notice. It had to be done even though she would miss this place and all the people here.

He leaned in and pecked her on the lips. "Okay honey. I have to finish payroll, so I'll be in the office if you need anything. Will you keep your eye open for any problems?"

"Of course baby."

Hayden was marking the board later in the night when the front door opened. She had never changed her desk, so she was always the first to see someone enter or leave. She was surprised when she saw Marcus Miller walk in.

She hoped that he wouldn't want his old job back. Mr. Fox would definitely squash that idea. Maybe he had just left some of his personal property behind and just wanted to pick it up. They hadn't thrown his personal effects out, but had kept them in a shoebox in Mr. Fox's office instead.

Marcus looked at her and then seemed surprised. His eyes quickly scanned her form leaving her a little uncomfortable.

"Hi Marcus." What did she say to a person that was carried out in handcuffs the last time she'd seen him? *Hope jail wasn't very bad... Why are you out already? Why are you here?*

He gave her a distracted look. "I see that fucker didn't waste no time replacing me did he?"

Hayden's mouth dropped.

"Low down dirty snitching dog... just low down." He muttered under his breath and then Hayden realized that Marcus was high on something.

"His own kid steals from him, but I do a little somthin' somthin' and he wants to send *me* to jail? Fuck him!" Marcus snapped and Hayden took a step backwards. He pimp walked across the aisle to Brian's old desk. Another employee was sitting there and she looked up in surprise.

"Where that motha fucker at?"

Hayden quickly backed out of the room. She darted to the office, her heartbeat slamming against her chest. She hurriedly opened the door and Brian looked up from the computer. The smile dropped from his face at her panicked expression.

"Brian! Marcus is out there and he's really messed up on something!"

Brian stood up just as loud shouting could be heard from the main room. Marcus was yelling and she could hear Abdullah's low voice, sounding as if he was trying to reason with him. There were times when people knew that their lives were about to permanently change, and in that second as she heard several people scream, Hayden knew that something horrible was about to happen and that it would forever change her.

Brian rushed forward just as the office door crashed open and Hayden turned in time to see Marcus standing in the door holding a gun. It was pointed at them! Fear froze her blood cold, but Brian was like a locomotive as he sprang forward. An explosion of sound engulfed her as Marcus repeatedly fired.

It took only one second from the time he appeared in the door firing the gun, until the angry sneer dropped from his face, replaced by one of surprise as Hayden was flung half around by the force of a bullet hitting her. She felt one brief punch in her chest that took her breath away and as she fell face first to the floor, she saw Brian's body fold. He was still trying to get to Marcus and she wanted to say *stop*. *Stop Brian, he's going to keep shooting you honey, stop...* but Hayden's world went black before she could say anything.

~Chapter 16~
A WONDERFUL CAPACITY FOR HEALING

"Hayden! Hayden!" She tried to open her eyes, but she was simply too tired. Oh! She had to get up and go to the gym.

In her mind, she pictured her dragging herself out of the bed and going through her familiar morning routine. She was pounding the treadmill, but it was too hard to breath. Damn, it was almost like running for the first time. In her mind, she climbed down and dropped to her knees trying to find her breath, but she couldn't.

Hayden clawed at her throat as she tried to gulp down a choking breath. Something was in her mouth and she couldn't breathe past it. She pulled it and felt a tube far back in her throat but hands quickly stopped her, gripping her wrists gently but firmly.

"Hayden! Doctor, someone, she's awake!"

Hayden blinked in panic as she tried to find her breath beyond the tube that was buried down her throat. Brian's pale face was there and the sight of it shocked her. He was holding her wrists and she wanted to explain that she couldn't breathe, that she was dying. Yet for some reason, he just looked happy.

Someone hurried into the room and a man dressed in a white lab coat stared into her eyes. "Cough Hayden. Cough and I'm going to pull out the breathing tube."

She tried to cough, but she still had no breath, however the tube was quickly pulled from her mouth in one swift but smooth motion and she immediately gulped down precious air.

"Good job," the man said. Now he was smiling too.

Brian released his firm grip on her wrists and he started to laugh as he stared at her. She didn't understand. Brian was laughing, but he didn't even look like the Brian she knew. His normally clean-shaven face now sported dark fuzz and his shaggy blonde hair was limp and in need of washing.

She couldn't speculate about it much though because she was still having trouble breathing. The man placed a mask to her nose and mouth and at first she tried to turn away until she felt the air. Then in a split second, it all came together for her.

She was in the hospital. She had been hurt... Brian had been shot!

She looked at his smiling face. He'd gotten shot. She tried to ask if he was okay, but her throat wouldn't allow even the faintest sound to escape.

He was holding her hands and he kissed them. "Everything is okay, honey. We're okay. We're okay." His gray eyes began to blur as unshed tears filled them, but even still, the smile remained on his face.

Hayden slept then, a normal dreamless sleep that helped to renew her body. When she awoke for the second time, she was aware of all that had happened, but she was much more surprised at what she was seeing than the realization that she had been shot. MyKell was sitting on her bed. He was staring at her. Her brow furrowed in shock.

"Hey," he said quietly. She just blinked at him in confusion. "You left me as one of your emergency contacts," he explained. "Your mom and dad too. They missed their first flight, but they should be here any time now." He continued to gaze at her. "You scared me Hade..." He cleared his throat. "I thought I'd lost you forever."

"Where...?" her voice wouldn't work. *Where is Brian?*

Brian came forward and sat on the other side of her bed. He reached for her hand and held it. She gave him a relieved smile and gripped his hand in return. MyKell's expression clouded and a moment later, he stood and retreated. Dani took his place before she gently rubbed Hayden's shoulder.

"You scared us all." She kissed Hayden's forehead. Then Hayden could see beyond her bed. The hospital room had several other people. Todd and Kia smiled at her from across the room and she smiled back. Dante was standing in the corner texting on his cell phone, and Mr. Fox was sitting in a chair looking like he had just awakened from a quick doze.

Hayden reached up and touched her sore throat. "How long...?" Ugh, it was hard to talk.

Brian responded. "You were just released from the ICU earlier today. You've been in the hospital for two days." He looked around. "Everyone that's been sitting in the waiting room finally got to come in to see you." There were chuckles.

"Not everybody," Todd said. "Kevin is still out there. He's a little..."

Tell him to come in, Hayden thought while giving Todd a piercing look.

Todd nodded. "Okay," then he left the room to get Kevin. Kia just looked confused by the silent communication. Hayden turned her attention back to Brian.

"Hurt?" was all that she could manage.

"I'm okay honey."

Mr. Fox spoke from across the room. "He was shot Hayden."

Brian gave him a disapproving look.

"She's a smart girl Brian. Tell her."

Brian sighed. "Marcus is in custody. He had gotten it into his head that my dad was behind the sting. So when he was released on bail bond, he got wasted and..." Hayden squeezed his hand letting him know that it was okay.

"He says that he wasn't trying to hurt you, Hayden. He wasn't even coming after me, but he was very wasted and thought he was shooting my... my dad. One bullet hit you in the chest. It cracked your ribs and settled in your left lung." Brian cleared his throat sounding upset.

Then Dani took over the story. "They did emergency surgery." She glanced over her shoulder. "Called him... MyKell to sign the release and they got that bullet out. You lost a lot of blood, so you did get a transfusion which is the only reason you were allowed to wake up."

"Brian?" Hayden asked, wanting to jump ahead to his injuries.

Brian took up the rest of the story. "I took a bullet to the side."

Hayden's hands squeezed into fists.

"It went completely through without hitting anything major."

"He was very lucky," Mr. Fox commented.

Brian nodded. "We both were. The bullet that hit you could have nicked your heart... my bullet could have hit my liver."

Mr. Fox stood and came forward. "I'm so sorry Hayden. You don't know how sorry I am about this happening to you-"

She shook her head firmly. *It's not your fault!* He just looked down, not accepting that.

He sighed. "Brian needs to rest."

"Dad!"

"Brian needs to be in bed," he continued.

Hayden met Brian's eyes. *I love you so much.*

"I love you too."

Rest. Get better. Do it for me.

He closed his eyes and then nodded.

Dani was plumping the pillows behind Hayden. She had been home for two days and since her mom and dad had left, Dani was filling in and babying her.

143

"MyKell called again."

"Ugh, no. What does he want?"

"You. I think your mama has been encouraging him too."

Hayden's eyes widened.

"Your mama is a trip. She asked what anybody knew about that 'White man'. Oh Hayden, I wanted to tell her so bad how much of a jack ass MyKell was, but I didn't. You should've told them that you had met someone else. They think Brian's just a stranger and your parents are calling either me or that fool about watching you."

"Oh my God, oh my God." Now she understood why MyKell kept calling; her parents had encouraged it!

"It's okay. They've gone home now. But you need to finish this with MyKell once and for all."

Hayden closed her eyes tiredly. "Hand me the phone."

His number was programmed into her phone—thanks to her mother who had done it one night when she had been knocked out on Vicodin. She called his cell number. He answered on the first ring.

"Hade? You okay?"

Ugh... she hated that nickname now.

"I'm okay. Hey, I thought you and I should have a talk. Would you come over?"

His hesitant response followed. "Sure. But everything is okay, right?"

She grimaced at his concern. "Yes. Can you come over at about five or six?" Brian would be over in the early evening and she did not want the two of them in the same room again.

There had already been some drama that developed over the last week, although it had resulted in some positive changes between Brian and Dani. Dani actually liked Brian now.

Hayden finished her brief conversation with MyKell and handed her phone back to Dani. As the pain in her chest began to intensify, she tried to find a comfortable position to relax against the pillows and a moment later the pain subsided.

"So he's coming over?" Dani asked. "You want me here? I'll mean mug his ass."

Hayden grinned. "You are crazy. I think I can handle him. I'm just not sure why he thinks that I'd have any interest in him at this point. I haven't even tried to contact him once in all this time. And I certainly haven't made any attempts to come on to him or to lead him on even if my Mama has been doing it for me." She shook her head in disbelief. "He's seen me hugged up with Brian, so where this is coming from is just crazy."

"Because some men only care about what *they* want. Check it out. He's willing to dump that woman he's with — the one he dumped you for, just to get you back now that he can't have you. He is a true loser!"

"I'm not disagreeing."

"Besides, I like the man you currently have."

Yes, Dani was now on Team Brian. On that first night in the ICU, Dani had been contacted because she was also listed as an emergency contact. However, only one person was allowed in the ICU with the patient. MyKell showed up and the two of them got into a heated argument. He thought he had a right because he had signed the consent, but Dani felt that she had all the rights because she was still included in Hayden's life.

Brian had gotten patched up and was still bloody, but he was adamant that he would be the one going into the ICU. MyKell's angry retort was cut short as Brian blew up. Dani said that Brian was nearly foaming at the mouth when he yelled that he had just taken a bullet and been sewed up twice and the only thing that was going to keep him out of that ICU was another bullet.

When MyKell tried to state that no one knew him, Brian had hollered that he was Hayden's future. For Dani that was it. She later told Hayden that if MyKell hadn't backed down, then Brian would have fought his old ass and won — even after taking a bullet to the gut mere hours before.

"Dani, why don't you go home? You've been here all day."

"Girl, don't be crazy. I am not going to leave you here alone with that fool. And someone should be here with you until Brian gets here. Besides..." She didn't finish the thought and Hayden gave her a curious look.

"What?"

She rolled her eyes and stopped fiddling with the bed sheets as she sat down. "I have zero desire to be at home. Dante makes me so sick. I know, I know. We talked about this, but I've finally realized that I dislike him much more than I like him."

"Oh?"

"Oh yeah. My best friend gets shot and he's worried about me not being home so he can get some ass! Plus, I found some pictures on his cell phone because he's too dumb to get rid of them... or else he just doesn't give a damn about me seeing them." Dani shook her head. "You don't need to hear my problems-"

"Yes I do. Are you okay Dani?"

Her friend shook her head. "No, but I just don't think about it. Dante's been in my life for so long, that I don't even know what it would be like not to have him always there anymore."

"Do you still love him?"

"I... don't think so. It's more anger now than anything else."

Hayden gripped her friend's hand. "I always wondered what if I had met Brian a year sooner, would we still have been together. But then I know that everything had to happen just the way it did so that Brian and I could be in the right place at the right time. Maybe that's what's happening to you now. Maybe you shouldn't regret the time you lost with Dante because it put you right where you needed to be."

Dani thought about that and then nodded. "I feel stupid for staying with him for so long though. But maybe it is how you say. I wasn't in the right time and place to let him go completely." She smiled. "Yeah."

"Are you there now?"

"I'm pretty sure that I am. And it's not about Sean either!"

Hayden smiled. "Are you going to tell Sean how you feel about him?"

Dani shook her head. "No. I need to fix myself first."

"Do *not* throw away a year of your life."

"Oh no girl. I can't go to the gym every day like you do."

MyKell didn't even wait until five before he showed up at Hayden's house. So he was most likely between jobs. Dani let him in because she exclaimed that she was not about to leave her best friend alone with a desperate ex-boyfriend. Hayden was more inclined to think that Dani was just nosey...

Hayden didn't really want to meet with MyKell in their old bedroom, but she was on strict bed rest while her surgical incisions healed., especially if she wanted to be well enough to attend the Zombie run at the end of the week. Plus Dani wouldn't let her go up and down the stairs, even though that was something they told pregnant women, not women who had suffered from a collapsed lung.

MyKell came into the room reeking of Issey Miyake cologne and wearing a pleather jogging suit and matching Kangol hat.

She tried not to look at him critically, but was still surprised that he had completely forgotten how much she disliked him in jogging suits. Especially since only old people wore them with Kangols...and why he thought that he should wear that expensive cologne she had bought him last Christmas as walking-around-daily cologne she was unsure but that was no longer her business. He leaned forward and kissed her cheek and she had to resist the urge to move her head away from his touch.

"You're looking very good Hade. In the hospital you had lost so much blood that you almost looked like a White woman." He sat down on the edge of her bed and smiled widely as if he'd just told a good one.

"Yeah. I... nearly died, so...yeah."

Ignoring her response he reached for her hand which she moved before he could touch her. This he pretended to ignore, too. "I'm happy you called me baby. I've been wanting to talk to you, but that friend of yours made that impossible. You know Hade; I could have been here to help you. I still can..."

She blinked in disbelief. "And your girlfriend? What would she think of that?" Hayden snapped.

"You're family Hayden. Gloria knows not to interfere with that. Besides..." he looked around the room, "...I miss you. I miss us. Gloria and I won't be together much longer."

He shook his head. "I messed up so badly by leaving. She nags and... well, I'm not going to complain about her, but I had it so good with you Hade." He reached for her hand again. "I know it was messed up how we ended, but sometimes relationships need a break."

Hayden immediately slipped her hand from his grasp. "You told me that things weren't right between us. That was honesty MyKell. I respected that.

"Things really weren't right between us. It took me some time to figure that out. And now that I have, I don't want to get back with you. My life is finally good just the way it is now."

A flash of anger crossed his face. "That White man, Brian. He's your new man?"

"Brian is my man."

MyKell removed his hat slowly and thought quietly. "Do you love him?"

"Very much so."

MyKell digested her words before he met her eyes again. "Is he good to you? He doesn't cheat on you or talk bad to you? He doesn't put his hands on you, does he?"

"No. He treats me like a queen."

MyKell sighed and then stood up. He replaced the hat on his head, but paused before leaving the room.

"Do I have even the slightest chance with you Hayden?"

"No," she said without a pause. "None."

"You look good baby," he said before he cleared his throat and then opened the door and left.

Hayden examined her feelings. Was there still something— anything, between her and MyKell? No, there wasn't; only a sense of awe that she had given up everything including her self-respect over *him*.

Hayden was dozing when she heard the front door open. Brian and Dani exchanged a few casual words and Hayden could tell that her friend had then left. Hayden struggled to sit up. The left side of her chest was sore as hell. The surgical site didn't even hurt as much as her chest did. During surgery, they had sealed the lung leak and all the air in the chest cavity had been drained, however she would be sore for at least several more weeks.

Of course that meant that she would miss running the marathon, but come hell or high water she was not going to miss rooting on her team. She still couldn't allow herself to think about all of that training and now she wouldn't even know if she could have done it or not. Hayden dismissed the thought and her disappointment as Brian entered her bedroom about fifteen minutes later carrying their dinner.

She hid a grimace as the aroma hit her. "Meatloaf and smothered cabbage?"

"Yep." He placed the tray on the bedside table and leaned forward to kiss her. Yesterday he had cooked dinner and wanted the instructions for her meatloaf and smothered cabbage. He had done an excellent job, but two days of cabbage was one day too many. Cabbage-induced flatulence was an ugly thing.

"I love this stuff," he said as he placed the folding tray before her and then began to eat from his own plate. Yesterday he had tried to feed her, but she turned her ahead away like a small child and said no, she could do it herself. He had laughed so deeply that the laughter spread to her, but only long enough for her to remember that laughter equaled excruciating chest pain.

"You're not eating your cabbage Hayden. You need your veggies to build your strength."

"Hmph. But I don't need gas at three A.M."

He shrugged. "I don't mind doing a Dutch oven with you."

She grimaced. "You better not put your head under the covers. That's gross."

"I think a man should know how horrible his woman's farts are."

"Okay, changing the subject... So how was work today?"

He paused and looked thoughtfully into the distance. "My dad says the office gives him the creeps. He wants to move out of Covington to a place in Cincinnati."

"Oh?"

"But I told him that it was a waste of money, so I'm not sure what his plans are. I think... he's just afraid."

She could understand that. There were days when she woke up in a cold sweat, even though she knew that Marcus hadn't been gunning for her or Brian. However, it was more the idea of how closely she had come to losing everything that caused her so many sleepless nights.

Marcus was in jail facing two counts of attempted murder. Upon sobering, he had been informed by the police themselves that Mr. Fox had nothing to do with the sting operation. In fact, several other sting operations had taken place at the same time. Marcus had immediately asked for Brian and Hayden's forgiveness. As of yet neither had been inclined to give it and now, he was facing life in prison over a misunderstanding.

Later that night, Brian climbed into her bed and then held her in his arms as they watched television. He was unusually quiet, but during a commercial he muted the sound. He stared at Hayden intently.

"That man was here – MyKell."

She was surprised at the intensity of his statement. "Yeah. I wanted to settle things once and for all."

"He...was up here, in your bedroom? And you weren't going to tell me?"

"Well... no. I mean, he's not even important enough to talk about-"

"Hayden, that's beside the point. That man still wants to be with you. He keeps hanging around waiting for a crumb to drop. I mean…why are you encouraging that?"

"Brian," she said in surprise. "I'm not. I told you already that MyKell means nothing and that's why he was over here. I told him to come so that I could tell him to get lost once and for all. Besides, how do you know he was here? Are you watching me, checking up on me or something?"

"No!" He sat up. "I can smell him and that fucking cologne that lingers on everything it comes in contact with." He gave her an accusatory look. "Including you."

"Brian! He kissed my cheek." She saw his teeth clench. "I just got shot in the lung. Do you really think I'm cheating on you?"

Brian shook his head. "No, of course I don't." He pulled Hayden back into his arms gently. "I'm sorry Hayden. I don't think that at all. But I know that your break up with him pushed you into a tail spin and so… I can understand if you still have some feelings for him."

"What?" She pulled away from him enough to cup his face between her hands. "Oh baby, I am so sorry. I should have… Brian I dislike MyKell so much that I can't believe that there was a time that I gave him even a second of my life. Baby, I'm in love with you and I have not led that man on. I told him today that he has no chance with me. None. Zilch. Zip. Fini… and whatever else means over and done with forever."

Brian kissed her swiftly. "Hayden I'm sorry. God, I'm such an asshole. I just accused the woman I love… Honey, I don't think you did anything wrong. I just worry that you might have some regrets about ending it with him. And if you did I would understand. I would kill him, but I would do so with great sadness."

"Brian, don't make me laugh," she pleaded while suppressing her laughter. "And no talk of killing. We've had enough of that."

"True." He slipped his tongue into her mouth. "My body misses yours," he groaned into her mouth. He reached up and cupped her breast but once he came into contact with her bandage he pulled back and lowered his hand.

"Oh God..." He panted and then moved to get out of bed. "I'm going to take a cold shower."

She reached out and stopped him. "Lay down honey."

He gave her a cautious, but hopeful look before complying. Hayden slipped her hand into his pajama bottoms and wrapped her warm fingers around his thick shaft.

Brian gasped and then closed his eyes. "Yes, baby, touch me... Oh damn Hayden!" His hips began to rock to the rhythm of her strokes. "God I missed you!"

Hayden pumped her fist up and down his shaft, using his slick pre-come as lube. She was becoming turned on, but didn't want to risk any heavy breathing. Still the sight of his purple cock was too delicious to disregard and so carefully, she leaned forward and worked her tongue around his swollen cockhead. As she tasted his sweet, yet salty semen, her mouth watered for more. Soon, she was leaning over him sucking, licking and deep throating this wonderful piece of him.

With a last grunt, Brian thrust upward, burying himself into her mouth and then pumped his come down her throat. "*Fuck!*" he screamed as his body spasmed. When his body stopped twitching in aftershocks, he rolled over onto his side, and looked at her.

"Are you okay?"

She smiled and nodded.

"I didn't hurt your chest did I?"

"No. You were delicious. My favorite dessert."

"Okay. We're going to try something. You stop me if it's too much."

She looked at him curiously. What was he up to?

He kissed her neck and her nipples instantly puckered impossibly hard. He knew just the right spot... His kisses moved lower until he was kissing the peak of each taut brown nipple.

Hayden's eyes rolled to the back of her head as she tried to regulate her breathing while keeping her body still. She wouldn't be able to hold it for long—she was already very turned on. "Touch me," she gasped.

As he lathed her nipples with his tongue, his fingers found her delicate folds and explored them expertly. Avoiding her bud, he slipped a finger into her warm canal and Hayden jerked and then relaxed. She regulated her breathing, but somehow, it made the experience all so much more heightened—trying to control herself to keep the sensations from taking over.

Brian's thumb brushed her bud and her body reacted, clenching and unclenching around his invading digit. She cried out as her honey flowed down his palm and coated his fingers. He fucked her with his finger; first one and then another, grazing her inner walls with the pads of his fingers with each stroke. She squeezed her toes tightly in order to stop her hips from rolling and pumping against his hand. Brian suddenly sucked her nipple hard and Hayden screeched and forgot all about her healing gunshot wound.

Dr. Abernathy paused before entering the office. He quirked his brow up at the sight of Hayden and Brian in zombie make-up. She grinned sheepishly.

"Sorry, we're on our way to the Zombie Run marathon."

"It's fine. This close to Halloween I see pretty much everything... usually not the walking dead, but there is a first time for everything."

Hayden had opted for old dead so she wore the white make-up with dark circles beneath her eyes. Brian wanted the freshly dead look so he had applied a mixture of ketchup and syrup to his clothes and neck.

Dr. Abernathy did his final medical check-up of Hayden and pronounced her to have a clean bill of health.

"Good luck young lady."

"We'll invite you to next year's Zombie Run," she said. "I'll be a fast running zombie which is so fake. Zombie's should be slow and do the 'grrrrr.'" Hayden lifted her hands and mimicked a Zombie.

Dr. Abernathy's smile faded. "Hayden... you won't be able to run a marathon. I mean, you might be able to engage in some light cardio, but you could never run anything like a long marathon."

Hayden felt hot and cold shivers running up and down her body and the world began to blink in and out of focus for her.

"Hayden, I thought you understood. Once your lung collapses then there is a high chance that it will happen again. I'm talking about spontaneous pneumothorax where you're just walking around and a bleb can break open out of nowhere."

"Yeah, but I just thought-"

"Hayden, if you push yourself like you would while running a marathon or engaging in intense cardio, then it will happen. That hole we repaired can always be compromised. I'm sorry."

She was stunned into silence and Brian just held her hand. His Zombie face was etched in sorrow.

So? she thought to herself. A collapsed lung wouldn't kill her... but it hurt really bad...

"Are you okay?" Brian asked as they drove to the marathon to root for Todd and Kevin.

"Let's just go home."

Brian gave her a surprised look before pulling the car over to the side of the road. He turned to her. "No. We're going to root our friends on. We're still Team Zombie."

She shook her head. "I can't."

"Hayden Michaels, I've never heard you say that *you can't.*"

"Brian, don't you understand that I can't even go to the gym now!" Her voice was thick with emotion and all she wanted to do was lie in her bed and cry. How could this be happening...?

"Baby steps honey."

She calmed down and when her breathing evened out again, she nodded. "My body is strong and healthy. I have a remarkable capacity for healing. Every function of my body operates exactly as it should," Hayden chanted to herself, creating her own affirmation.

"Yes," Brian agreed as he whipped out his cell phone. He was repeating her words to himself and typing them into his phone.

"You say this every day until your body knows it's true." He pulled the car back out onto the road and drove them to the marathon.

~EPILOGUE~
OCTOBER 30, 2013

Hayden warmed up. She was wearing lycra running pants that hugged every curve, pronounced every dimple in her thighs and that barely held in the pooch of her belly. None of it bothered her because the added weight had come to her honestly and for a good cause. Plus, she knew what to do to rid herself of it – but all in due time.

Dani looked scared. "I don't think I can do this," she whimpered.

"Yeah, you can. I trained you myself and I know you got this."

Dani nodded. In the last year she had lost most of her extra weight and what was left was toned and tight.

"Boys! That's enough!" Todd yelled. Kevin and Adrian were arguing because Kevin insisted that his brother couldn't dress like a super hero during a Zombie Run.

"But Dad, that's stupid!" Kevin exclaimed. He was tall, thin and already a track star at his high school.

"Kevin, your brother can wear what he wants. Now start your warm up."

"I don't need to warm up," he pouted.

"Fine. I guess I'll out run you again this year."

"Ha! No you won't. This is my year to beat you Dad."

"We'll see about that."

Brian strolled over to Hayden. His zombie makeup had evolved to now being a zombie hunter and everyone did a pretty good job at guessing that he was Daryl Dixon from the show *The Walking Dead*. It helped that he carried an unloaded automatic crossbow and that he had great biceps in his sleeveless shirt.

They exchanged quick kisses. "You're kissing the enemy," she joked. She was a long dead zombie with skeletal make-up.

"You wouldn't have been the enemy if you had dressed like Michon like I wanted."

"I am not wearing that bad Rasta, dreadlock wig."

"Sweetheart, you can't have great looking dreds during the Zombie Apocalypse. Right, Dani?"

Dani laughed. "Brian this is Team Zombie not Team Zombie Killers."

"Where's my child?" Hayden asked.

"Dad's holding her."

Hayden looked over at the sidelines where Mr. Fox was sitting in a foldout chair bouncing his granddaughter on his knee. They were surrounded by several of their friends from Fox and Fox Vinyl—the name Bob had renamed the company once he moved the office to Cincinnati. Among them was his pretty wife who looked bored and out of place in spiked heels and dangling earrings. Pam and Abdullah were there, as well as several others from the office. Their friend Bill was leaning against his car having a smoke so as not to offend the non-smokers. Although he had kicked his drug addiction he still smoked like a chimney— something Brian was trying to help him curtail.

The youngest member of the Fox family kicked fat legs and gurgled happily at her grandpa who was talking to Sean, Dani's man. Sean was still a great catch; tall, dark, handsome, no children, but now he was no longer single. Luckily, the attraction Dani had felt towards Sean was mutual and after unlatching herself from Dante, Sean became a tremendous support system and then later, he became much more.

Little Serenity Fox was four months old and her mom didn't know if it would be possible to train for the Zombie Run in just four short months. Serenity's dad made sure that her mom did not over-do it and Auntie Dani kept Hayden active during her pregnancy by being her first client as a personal trainer. Hayden had long ago given up her two jobs in order to be a stay at home mom and to indulge in her love for fitness as well as her love for self-affirmations. Daily, Hayden blogged positive affirmations and was pleased to see the positive response she got from them.

She also worked in tandem with Todd as a personal training team. When one wasn't able to work, the other would step in. It was mutually beneficial, allowing each time with their families, while also giving Hayden an opportunity to go to the gym without engaging in strenuous exercise. She had yet to suffer a reoccurrence of a collapsed lung, but that didn't mean it would never happen again.

Kia was holding the hand of her and Todd's little one as she joined the group to wish them good luck. Jordan was just learning to walk and Todd was convinced that his son was a genius because he was only ten months old. He scooped up the toddler who gave his Zombie make up an unsure look before straining to be put down.

Hayden wondered again at the strangeness of her life. Both she and Kia had given birth to biracial children. Serenity was gray-eyed with red hair and barely any brown to her skin, while Jordan was even more brown than Kia, although he looked just like Todd. Or what Todd would look like if he were African American.

Serenity had Hayden's features though, and through her daughter, Hayden was able to see more of the beauty within herself. Well, she would never doubt that beauty again. She remembered an affirmation that Brian had sent her long ago... something about: "It is through your eyes that I realize the extent that I can be loved..."

"Runners, head to your positions!"

Brian gave her another kiss. "Good luck honey. You have your cell phone in case something happens?"

"Yes."

"And I'll be with her every step of the way," Dani added.

Brian nodded once and then retreated, nervous but not wanting to fill his wife with any self-doubt. Team Zombie stood ready at the starting line. They had grown from three to twelve, including several people from Fox and Fox; Abdullah's kids, as well as Raina, Bill's wife and the team's youngest member who stood at the ready wearing a cape and a super hero costume.

Danyelle had a determined look on her face as they waited for the whistle to blow. "Thirty miles is a long way to run."

"No one said we had to run the entire thing. We can run some and walk some."

"We can?"

"We can do whatever we set our minds to do."

Brian carried their sleeping daughter into the house. They had just barely moved in by the time Serenity was born. It had been a mad rush against time to be settled in before they welcomed the newest addition to their family.

Hayden had sold her old house without a second thought. By that time, she and Brian had already been married for two months and baby Serenity was already brewing in her mommy's tummy. Their wedding night was the second time that Brian had made love to her without a condom. Her daughter was a wedding night conception—though she would never tell Serenity that story, although her daughter would probably figure it out on her own.

Brian watched his wife limp into the house. "Are you going to need me to carry you, too?" he joked.

"No, if you just put the baby to bed and run me a hot bath, I would be mighty appreciative."

"You got it." Before he headed up the stairs, he kissed Hayden gently. "You did good honey. I'm proud of you. I'm sorry you didn't win."

"Well, there's always next year for Team Zombie. And maybe next year, you'll actually run the marathon with us."

He shook his head. "Nah, I like signing autographs. For once in history, being a redneck is cool."

"Yeah well, take advantage of it," she advised, implying that it wouldn't last forever.

He swatted her rump and then headed up the stairs.

Hayden kicked off her shoes and then stooped and placed them neatly in the closet. Her back creaked, but it wasn't all together unpleasant. She headed for the office that she and Brian shared; he used it for his work with Fox and Fox, and she used it for writing her daily affirmations blog.

She'd just thought of one that she didn't want to lose. So sinking into the leather office chair, she powered up her laptop and gazed at the photograph of the three of them posing for their first family portrait. Sometimes, just looking at the picture gave her so many affirmations. However, today her joy was due to completing a hard task.

Dani hadn't copped out and had continued until she limped past the finish line. Although Kevin hadn't beat his dad, he had won a metal in the teen age group, while Todd had placed third over all. Hayden had come in 23rd overall, and 10th in the women's category. She was pretty damn proud of herself.

She logged into her website: *Now Repeat After Me—Your Link to Daily Affirmations.* She read the comments of some of her followers, smiling when a particularly good one found its place in a reader's heart. Then she began typing tomorrow's affirmation: "I need not know the entire journey in order to take the first step."

The End

"I don't allow the harshness of others or the world around me to harden the softness that lives inside me. It is my softness that helps to heal my world…"

-Pep's Affirmation

PEPPER PACE BOOKS
~~***~~

STRANDED!
Juicy
Love Intertwined Vol. 1
Love Intertwined Vol. 2
Urban Vampire; The Turning
Urban Vampire; Creature of the Night
Urban Vampire; The Return of Alexis
Wheels of Steel Book 1
Wheels of Steel Book 2
Wheels of Steel Book 3
Wheels of Steel Book 4
Angel Over My Shoulder
CRASH
Miscegenist Sabishii
They Say Love Is Blind
Beast
A Seal Upon Your Heart
Everything is Everything Book 1
Everything is Everything Book 2
Adaptation
About Coco's Room

SHORT STORIES
~~***~~

Someone to Love
The Way Home
MILF
Blair and the Emoboy
Emoboy the Submissive Dom
1-900-BrownSugar
Someone To Love
My Special Friend

Baby Girl and the Mean Boss
A Wrong Turn Towards Love
The Delicate Sadness
The Shadow People
The Love Unexpected

COLLABORATIONS
~~***~~

Seduction: An Interracial Romance Anthology Vol. 1
Scandalous Heroes Box set

About the Author

Pepper Pace creates a unique brand of Interracial/multicultural erotic romance. While her stories span the gamut from humorous to heartfelt, the common theme is crossing racial boundaries.

The author is comfortable in dealing with situations that are, at times, considered taboo. Readers find themselves questioning their own sense of right and wrong, attraction and desire. The author believes that an erotic romance should first begin with romance and only then does she offers a look behind the closed doors to the passion.

Pepper Pace lives in Cincinnati, Ohio where many of her stories take place. She writes in the genres of science fiction, youth, horror, urban lit and poetry. She is a member of several online role-playing groups and hosts several blogs. In addition to writing, the author is also an artist, an introverted recluse, a self proclaimed empath and a foodie. Pepper Pace can be contacted at her blog, Writing Feedback:

http://pepperpacefeedback.blogspot.com/

PepperPace.tumblr.com or by email at
pepperpace.author@yahoo.com

Awards

Pepper Pace is a best selling author on Amazon and AllRomance e-books as well as Literotica.com. She is the winner of the 11th Annual Literotica Awards for 2009 for Best Reluctance story, as well as best Novels/Novella. She is also recipient of Literotica's August 2009 People's Choice Award, and was awarded second place in the January 2010 People's Choice Award. In the 12th Annual Literotica Awards for 2010, Pepper Pace won number one writer in the category of Novels/Novella as well as best interracial story. Pepper has also made notable accomplishments at Amazon. In 2013 she twice made the list of top 100 Erotic Authors and has reached the top 10 best sellers in multiple genres as well as placing in the semi-finals in the 2013 Amazon Breakthrough Author's contest.

Made in the USA
Monee, IL
01 November 2020